HOME SICK

JESSICA L. HARRIS

Home Sick © 2013 Jessica L. Harris

ISBN: 978-0-9894137-0-1

Book Design by Lora Morgenstern
Headshot by Lora Morgenstern
Makeup: Talia Culley

Front Cover, Girl: istockphoto.com/OSTILL
Front Cover, Empire State Photo: istockphoto.com/stu99
Back Cover: istockphoto.com/narkorn
City Icon: Juan Pablo Bravo,
Building Icon: Antonis Makriyannis,
from The Noun Project
Empire State Building Icon by Kenneth Appiah

DEDICATION

*To my best friend- the best selling author
of all time who blessed me with the talent to write
this book. Your love is perfect. Jesus I love you
with all my heart. Thank you for all you've
blessed me with.*

Mother To Son

Don't you fall now—
For I'se still goin', honey,
I'se still climbin',
And life for me ain't been no crystal stair.

— Langston Hughes

PROLOGUE

My nose ran faster than my feet could. Like my nose, my toes were numb. New York winters had no mercy. It attacked me, a poor, defenseless child. Its cold wind stung so much it burned. The freezing temperature paralyzed my muscles like the venom of a jellyfish.

"Damn, you're slow," my mother yelled as I struggled to climb the stairs that ran through Jackie Robinson Park. We were walking to Edgecombe Avenue, which was at the top of Sugar Hill. Unlike its name, what waited for me at the top of those steps damn sure wasn't sweet.

I stopped to catch my breath. The stairs were steep. There had to be at least a hundred of them. It was enough to knock the wind out of the strongest athlete. By step ninety-nine, my frail, six-year-old body was beyond deflated.

I hunched over, placing one hand on my thigh. The other held the talking teddy bear my grandmother had given me three months before as a Christmas present. It was the last present I would ever receive from my grandmother. She didn't live to see another Christmas. Her heart stopped beating just short of Valentine's Day.

I considered sitting down but was afraid. It was pitch black. I heard glass crunch beneath my feet. Scary voices moaned indecipherable words. Even the trees spoke, their branches crying out in protest when the wind blew.

My mother looked back at me and screamed, "Damn it, Tangia!" She ran to me, grabbed my wrist, and lifted me off the ground. I thought my shoulder would pop out of its socket. I tightened my grip on Teddy.

"Ow," I cried out. She ignored me. Like a ragdoll, I was swung across the street. She put me down at the entrance of what appeared to be an abandoned building.

I stood still. My mother didn't. Her entire body twitched. She looked uneasy, as if she were anticipating something. She spoke to a man at the entrance of the building.

"What you got?" he asked.

She pulled $5 worth of food stamps out of her back pocket and slapped it into the man's hand. She bit her nails as she waited for a response. They were dirty and bitten down past the skin. It looked as if she'd been nibbling on the pads of her fingertips. They started to bleed.

"It's not enough," he said. "What else you got?"

She glanced at me but fixed her eyes on Teddy. I pulled him into my chest, hugging him as tight as my numb fingers would allow.

"I got this," she said, trying to pry the bear from my fingers.

"No!" I screeched in protest.

"Let go!" she screamed back.

"No. Get off of me, Keyshia!" I yelled as loud as I could. My voice cracked.

My mother pushed me to the ground. I landed on my hip bone.

"Ah!" I yelled. I let go of Teddy and pulled my knees into my chest, hoping it would dull the pain. My mother grabbed the teddy bear and handed it to the man. I looked up at her. She tapped her foot and pulled at the ends of her hair.

"A teddy bear?"

"Hold on it…it talks," she stuttered, pushing the button in the bear's back.

"Teddy loves you," Teddy said. She pushed the button again. "Teddy thinks you're special." She pushed the button one last time. "You're my best friend."

My chest ached as Teddy spoke the words that were meant for me to a total stranger.

The man inspected the bear and looked back at my mother.

"And there's something else I can give you," she told the man.

I didn't have anything else, and neither did my mother, but somehow, the man knew what she was talking about.

"Follow me," he said, smirking. "But the kid has to stay out here."

My mother followed the man and didn't look back.

I stood up. There was a shallow ditch in front of the adjacent building. It was surrounded by bricks and covered by scaffolding. I climbed into the ditch and lay down. The ground was cold and hard. I tried to look up at the sky, but my tears and the scaffolding blocked my view. I wiped my eyes and walked across the street. I lay down on a bench where I could see the sky.

Before my grandmother died, she promised me that she'd watch over me from heaven. If I stayed under the scaffolding, she wouldn't be able to see me. So, I stayed on the bench. Knowing that my grandmother always kept her promises, I felt safe and fell asleep.

1

BACK IN THE CITY

{PRESENT DAY}

"Port Authority."

I jumped at the sound of the bus driver's voice.

I took a deep breath and tried to calm down. My hands trembled as I reached for the duffel bag under my feet. I didn't plan on staying long, so I packed light.

I hadn't been home since the semester started. There was a reason for that. I didn't miss my family, I didn't miss the friends I didn't have, and I damn sure didn't miss my neighborhood.

The thought of home caused a nervous twitch to consume my arms, fingers, legs, and toes. I rubbed the palms of my hands against the seat of the bus so hard that they felt as if they had flames beneath them.

Exiting the bus, I was met by a woman begging for change.

"Change, please?" she asked.

"Thanks for reminding me," I said, throwing nothing in her cup and tightening the grip on my bag.

I was a New Yorker again. It wasn't like I ever stopped being one, but the panhandler reminded me of the heightened sense of awareness I needed now that I was back in the city.

In New York, even people who have nowhere to go have to get there fast — including me. I was in no rush to get home but sped up to keep pace with the people shooting past me.

As I walked, I thought of the route I'd take to get home. I could take the A-train to 145th Street and then take the bus to 155th. Or, I could walk a couple of blocks to 6th Avenue and hop on the D-train, which stopped right in front of my building. The less walking I had to do in my neighborhood, the better, so I decided to take the D.

I stepped outside the bus, and there was everything I didn't miss over the last four months — Times Square. Even at eleven PM, it looked like the sun was out on 42nd Street. After pushing through the first crowd of tourists a quarter of a block from the bus station, I regretted walking to the D. It was Christmas time, and the streets were infested with tourists. To them, every tall building was amazing, every bright light put a sparkle in their eyes, and every step was another photo op. After saying excuse me about a dozen times, I decided to let my body do the talking and push.

My eyes caught quick glimpses of posters with names drawn in pastel-colored flowers and pretty birds by Chinese vendors. The examples hanging from the carts always displayed names like Jessica and Michael. They were never Seniqua or Leroy.

My face was met by steam from the street meat truck that I always tried to avoid in fear of smelling like Abdul's shish kebobs or Mohammad's hot dogs. At the corner, a man pounded on the bottoms of buckets with a set of drumsticks. I danced around the smelly smoke, crossed the street, and descended into the depths of the train station.

Because it was late, I ended up waiting for the train for close to twenty-five minutes. I'd taken my last final two days before, so I had no textbook to read or paper to work on. To pass the time, I pulled out a book I'd been reading for most of the bus ride from school. It was an anthology of African American and Latino poetry. I turned to a poem by Julia Alvarez. My eyes ran across the words on the page, but unlike the gum on the post I stood next to, nothing stuck.

When I stepped onto the car of the train, my nose burned. A smell radiated off a homeless woman who looked like she hadn't bathed in months. She wore a knit hat that looked more dirt grey than white, multiple layers of knit sweaters, and black spandex tights that were covered in tiny balls of lint. Pieces of her matted hair escaped through the holes in her hat the same way her big toe did from her torn sneaker. She was slumped over, sleeping, with a cardboard sign that read *I'm Hungry. Please Help. God Bless* slipping through her dirty, dry fingers. Duane Reade bags filled with old newspapers, paper towels, and other random things laid around her feet like presents around a Christmas tree. Her breathing was heavy as if the air in her lungs was dying to escape and make its way into a cleaner vessel. Not wanting it to choose mine, I ran for the door.

"Damn it!" I yelled as the doors shut in my face. I stood right where I was, so I could run to the next car at the next stop. I attempted, unsuccessfully, to hold my breath. I glanced around the car of the train. How had I not noticed that I'd stepped into an almost empty car? That's always a warning sign. If a car of a train is empty in a New York City subway, it's either because it has no A.C. or heat, the doors are broken, or someone is stinking it up. I'd rather die freezing than from B.O. suffocation. I saw the woman's head pop up in the reflection of the window. She stood up and walked toward me.

"I don't have any money," I said, tightening the grip on my bag.

She leaned over my shoulder and whispered into my ear. "He who dwells in the shelter of the Most High will rest in the shadow of the Almighty. He will cover you with his feathers, and under his wings, you will find refuge. If you make the Most High your dwelling, then no harm will befall you. No disaster will come near your tent, for He will command His angels concerning you to guard you in all your ways."

As quickly as she said it, she walked away. The words themselves were strangely beautiful, but assuming they were from the Bible, I wrote them off as nonsense. Obviously, her belief wasn't doing much for her. My house was pretty bad, but it was better than a train. If she believed the words she spoke, why was she homeless and living on a train?

Finally, the train arrived at the next stop. I ran to the next car, which smelled much better, and took a seat.

It was a little after midnight. I took out my calendar and crossed off December 15th. The day was officially over. There were thirty seven days before I could leave New York and head back to school.

I took out my iPod and threw on my headphones as a sign to the other passengers on the train to leave me alone. I scrolled through my playlist, sucked my teeth, and sighed.

I had Stephen's iPod.

I remembered the day it happened. I'd looked up from my psychology book. Stephen took his earphones out and motioned for me to do the same.

"Let's switch." He smiled, extending his hand and the iPod toward me.

"What for?" I took my second earphone out.

"Break up the monotony a little."

"No one said studying was supposed to be fun, Stephen."

"Come on, Gia. Live a little," he said, dropping his iPod onto my textbook.

I shrugged my shoulders, said, "All right," and handed him my iPod. I scrolled through his playlist as he scrolled through mine.

"What do you know about Luther Vandross, Gia?" he asked, smiling, putting my earphones in, and pressing a button. He sang along to *"A House is not a Home"*, obviously unable to hear himself.

"Stephen, shush," I said putting my finger over my mouth, looking around to see if he'd disturbed anyone.

We were in the stacks of the library, surrounded by books. And, with the millions of words they had at their disposal, they didn't say as much as one to tell Stephen to shut up.

I continued to scroll through his playlist. John Mayer. I chose a song called *"Daughters"*, took out my highlighter, and continued studying. I tapped my foot to the song's lighthearted melody and stopped highlighting to listen to the lyrics.

Out of the corner of my eye, I saw a guy sitting across from me mouthing something, which I assumed was stupid but couldn't hear. I avoided eye contact. He stood up and hit his head on the metal bar that hung over the seat. I looked down and tried not to laugh but couldn't help it. He sat next to me and tapped me on the leg. I took the earphone out of my right ear and gave him the *what is it* look.

"What's so funny, ma?"

"Nothing's funny. Nothing." I crossed my arms, hoping he would get the point.

"Oh, word? Well, that's cool. What you listening to?" He looked to be about twenty-five. He was handsome, well-dressed, neat, and clean. Still, I wasn't interested.

"John Mayer. You know him?" I knew he wouldn't. It was a great way to end the conversation and get back to minding my own business. And hopefully, he would mind his.

"Oh yeah? Ain't that the dude who was on the *Dave Chappelle Show*?"

My plan failed. I forgot about that episode of the *Chappelle Show*. Dave Chappelle and John Mayer's social experiment. I almost laughed thinking of it but stopped myself, knowing that the man sitting next to me would mistake my laugh for an invitation to keep talking.

"Yeah, that's him," I fidgeted with the buttons on the iPod.

"You into that white music?" he asked. I rolled my eyes and turned my back toward him. "*Hello,*" he said, obviously not getting the point, so I decided to turn it up a notch.

"Listen. I'm indubitably enervated. I fancy listening to my technological muse rather than your balderdash. So, if it suits you, I'd prefer to recoil to my *Caucasian music.*"

"I don't know what all that means, but I do know that you're beautiful. Is there some way I can keep in touch with you?" He was not going to give up.

"No. There's not." I got straight to the point.

"I'm sayin'. You ain't got no phone?"

"No. I *don't have* a phone," I said, correcting his grammar.

"Well, let me give you my number, and you can–"

I cut him off. "No."

"*What?*" He raised his eyebrows. I assumed that meant I needed to make it a little clearer. The couple of months I'd spent in Rhode Island must have softened me up. This guy reminded me that things worked a little differently here.

"Are you *deaf?* I'm *not interested,*" I said in a loud, slow voice, moving my hands and pretending to use sign language. A couple of people on the train started laughing. He looked around. Knowing they were laughing at his failed attempt to get my telephone number, he was embarrassed and retaliated.

"Aight, shorty. It's like that? You ain't all that anyway," he laughed, looking around the train to make sure he could be heard. "You probably don't even like black dudes. Listening to John Mayer." He laughed again, hoping someone would join him. No one did.

"That's where you're wrong. I like black men. I just don't like *you*." More laughs echoed from people on the train.

"You ain't all that anyway."

"Really?" I asked. "Was I all that five minutes ago when you were trying to get my number?" More laughs.

"59th Street. Columbus Circle," the conductor announced over the loudspeaker.

"Whatever, man." He got off of the train. I put my headphones back on. As John Mayer played the guitar, I thought of my room back at school, Stephen, and everything else about Brown University that I was already missing after only the first day of being away. I sat trying to calculate a way to go back the day after Christmas.

2

UPTOWN

As the train approached 145th Street, the conductor made an announcement. "This train will not stop at the 155th Street station."

"Damn it," I said under my breath. Now, I had to get off at 145th Street and either take the bus or a cab or walk home. I didn't want to waste the little amount of money I had on a $6 cab ride to go ten blocks. Because it was late, the bus would mean standing outside in the freezing cold waiting. I decided to walk.

I walked down Bradhurst Avenue because there were too many people on 8th, especially at this time of night. At the end of Bradhurst, I turned on 155th. Once I reached the corner, I knew I was officially home.

Home, bittersweet home. Home was where my heart wasn't. Police sirens polluted the air. Groups of men littered the sidewalks and hustled in front of corner stores. Kennedy's Fried Chicken was packed with people looking to satisfy their late-night munchies. The neighborhood drunks and crack addicts staggered around, looking for their next hits. I walked looking down, hoping they wouldn't ask me for money.

I grew up in the Polo Ground Projects in Harlem. The neighborhood had changed since I was younger but still had its issues. During the eighties and early nineties, crack cocaine did its damage. The effects of its withdrawal could still be seen.

As usual, the elevator smelled of urine and cigarettes. I considered joining the swim team at school because I'd become an expert at holding my breath during the ride from the first to the twenty-sixth floor. Too bad I couldn't swim.

Music blasted into the hallway from nearby apartments. Unidentified fried foods added to the smell of urine and cigarettes. I got to my door, put my bag down, and took a deep breath, preparing myself for what was on the other side. I had a key but was afraid of what I might see if I opened the door unannounced. I cracked my neck, rotated my shoulders, and rang the bell.

"Who?" a groggy voice from the other side of the door asked.

"Keyshia, it's me. Gia." I heard her gasp as she quickly unchained and unlocked the door.

"Tangia!" my mother screamed. She threw her frail arms around me. I stood with mine to my sides. I peeked over her back to get a glimpse of the apartment — filthy as usual. There were empty beer bottles on the kitchen counter. The sink was full of cereal bowls half filled with sour milk. Dirty clothes hung over the arms of the couch. And, of course, there were the roaches.

My mother stepped away and grabbed my arms, looking me up and down.

"Tangia, look at you! You put on weight. Good weight."

I couldn't say the same about her. She wore a stained, pink satin nightgown that came just above her knees.

One of its spaghetti straps fell down past her bony shoulder and rested on the track marks at the hinge of her arm. Her bones protruded from her neck and chest. Her arms looked like tree branches, and her hands were dry and cracked. Her nails were bitten down past the skin. My eyes widened as I noticed her belly.

"You're pregnant!" I yelled, forgetting I was standing in the middle of the hallway.

"Child, get inside. Screamin' like that!"

I picked up my bags and walked into the living room. A man in a dirty white undershirt sat on the couch, drinking a cheap beer.

"And who the hell are you?" I asked.

"Tangia! What they teaching you? Rudeness up in that college?" I backed away when I smelled the alcohol on her breath.

"Who is he? And when the hell did you get pregnant, Keyshia?"

"You let her call you Keyshia like that?" The man set his beer on the coffee table.

"Who are you?" I demanded, dropping my bag.

"If you bothered to call or come home for Thanksgiving, you would have known," she said.

"Unbelievable." I grabbed my bag and stormed to my room. The plaques hanging from the walls shook when I slammed the door. I fell onto the bed, put my hands under my head, leaned against a propped pillow, and looked at the awards. They were dusty and needed to be cleaned. When my grandmother was alive, she hung them in her apartment and dusted them every day. I hated that she wouldn't be able to do the same with my college diploma.

I pulled my book out of my purse and reread the Julia Alvarez poem I attempted to read in the train station.

Ironing Their Clothes[1]
With a hot glide up, then down, his shirts,
I ironed out my father's back, cramped
And worried with work. I stroked the yoke,
The breast pocket, collar and cuffs,
Until the rumpled heap relaxed into the shape
Of my father's broad chest, the shoulders shrugged off
The world, the collapsed arms spread for a hug.
And if there'd been a face above the button-down neck,
I would have pressed the forehead out, I would
Have made a boy again out of that tired man!
If I clung to her skirt as she sorted the wash
Or put out a line, my mother frowned,
A crease down each side of her mouth.
This is no time for love! But here
I could linger over her wrinkled bed jacket,
Kiss at the damp puckers of her wrists
With a hot tip. Here I caressed collars, scallops, ties, pleats
Which made her outfits test of the patient of my passion.
Here I could lay my daydreaming iron on her lap.
The smell of baked cotton rose from the board
And blew with a breeze out the window
To the family wardrobe drying on the clothesline,
All needing a touch of my iron.
Here I could tickle
The underarms of my sister's petticoat
Or secretly pat the backside of her pajamas.
For she too would have warned me not to muss
Her fresh blouses, starched jumpers, and smocks,
all that my careful hand had ironed out,
Forced to express my excess love on cloth.

I woke up and noticed I'd fallen asleep in my clothes. I

rummaged through my bag and grabbed my pajamas and tooth-brush. I glanced at the clock — four AM. I went to the bathroom to brush my teeth. The combination of my toothbrush and the sound of my mother's headboard banging against the wall of the bathroom caused me to gag.

"Sick bastard. She's pregnant," I shouted, banging on the wall with my fist. The banging stopped. As quickly as the question came of who my future sibling's father was, it left. I decided I didn't care. If the baby actually lived, Social Services would take it anyway.

I woke up at seven AM. I was thankful that my mother and her *friend* were still asleep. I took a shower, ate some cereal, and headed for the Youth Center.

I needed to make some money and keep busy over the break. While I was in high school, I worked at the Youth Center on 129th Street. I helped elementary school-aged kids with their homework and played games with them. I wanted to get to the Center the second it opened, nine AM sharp. The less time spent at my mother's apartment, the better.

When Gladys saw my face peeking through the window, she screamed and ran to the door.

"Hi, Gladys."

"Gia!" she exclaimed as she hugged me. "Let me get a good look at you, girl. You look even more beautiful, if that's possible. This might sound silly, but you look smarter too."

We both laughed, and I realized there were some things I actually did miss about New York. "So, how'd you do?" she asked.

"Well, I just took my last final a couple of days ago. So, I'll have to wait a little while to get my grades. But, I know I did well."

"I knew you would. I'm so proud of you. So, what's up? What brings you here so early in the morning?"

"I was hoping you'd have a job for me."

"Well, funding for the Center has really been cut back. But, there's always room for my Gia. I can give you two days a week, two PM to six PM, and call you in as a sub if needed. Oh, and the Center will be closed Christmas Eve till January 2nd."

I looked around the Center. I didn't think it was possible for it to look worse than it did when I left. The dull red paint looked like chipped nail polish as it peeled off the surface of the concrete walls. The carpet was tattered and dingy. The ceiling panels were stained brown from leaks. Some were missing, exposing corroded pipes covered in cobwebs. Hooks were missing from the cubbies where the children hung their coats and book bags. The tables where they did their homework wobbled, and the plastic chairs that sat around them were cracked.

"Okay. That'll work. Can I start today?" I was hoping to get more hours but decided to take what I could get.

"The kids are going to be so excited to see you."

I spent the morning at the Center, even though I wasn't getting paid until two. I filled Gladys in on all the details of my first semester. She gave me the latest update on what was going on at the Center and around the neighborhood.

Thoughts of my pregnant mother and the living conditions I'd be forced to endure for the next month faded the moment the children walked through the door.

"Gia!" they screamed as they ran to me. "We missed you!"

"I missed you too." Thirty pairs of hands and feet grabbed and surrounded me. Most of the kids who came to the Center went to school nearby and lived in the area. It was a government-subsidized after-school program that was part of Welfare to Work. The Center provided free child care to women participating in the program while they worked. It was unfortunate but typical that spending for the program was being cut.

"Where you been, Gia?" one of the boys asked. He was one of my favorites. He was in fourth grade and was very intelligent.

"Put your coat away, get your homework out, and I'll tell everyone about my first semester in college."

"College?" His eyes lit up as he ran to put away his coat and take out his homework. "Hurry up, ya'll," he said to the other kids. "Gia's gonna tell us about college." It took a second for the kids to get settled. Once they did, Gladys addressed the group.

"Get your homework out, and get in your seats. Ya'll better stop acting like you don't know how to act up in here," Gladys said, trying to get the kids under control. She waited with her arms crossed in front of her chest, while the kids took their seats and quieted down. "All right, now. So, we have a special visitor with us today. Gia's back."

"Yeah!" the kids screamed. Some even got out of their seats. Gladys shot them a stern look. They returned to their seats and were quiet.

"Now, if you all would just *act right*, before we start homework, Gia is going to talk to us about college. Gia, you ready?" She turned to me and asked.

I nodded. "Hey, everyone. I just came back from my first semester at college."

"Gia, what's a semester? And what college did you go to?" one of the children asked.

"I go to Brown University. It's in Rhode Island, a couple of hours away from here. And a semester is a period of time you are in college — usually about four months. I had to study very hard in high school to get into college. And, now that I'm in college, I have to study even harder. When I graduate, I can get a good job and make a lot of money. Who wants to go to college?"

"Meeeee!" the students shouted in unison, raising their hands.

"I wanna make a lot of money," a boy said in a low voice to no one in particular.

"Good. So, let's get started on that homework." I laughed as they threw open their books.

"I don't know about you, but I'm going to college," the same boy whispered to another sitting next to him.

3

ROLLING STONES

I came back to an empty apartment and refrigerator. The only thing I found was milk that expired the previous day. When I was a little girl, my mother sold our food stamps to buy drugs. By the looks of the fridge, old habits died hard.

Toward the end of the semester, I overheard the white girls at school talking about the *freshman fifteen* they gained over the course of the semester, and how they planned on losing it over the winter break. When there was no food to eat and no money to buy food, losing weight wasn't all that hard.

After smelling the milk and deciding it was okay to drink, I ate a bowl of cereal and went to my room. Clothes were thrown all over the place, and my bag was turned inside out. I'd been away from home long enough to forget my mother was a junkie. She tore through my bag looking for money. Like an idiot, I left a $100 bill in it. Luckily, I had another $100 in my wallet that I had taken with me to the Center.

I threw my clothes back into the bag, bundled up, and headed for the payphone on the corner. I called my older brother, Micah. Micah was my father's son, not my mother's. I met him at my father's funeral when I was fourteen and he was nineteen. We were the only two of our father's six children who went. Although I knew very little about my father's other children, I knew I was my father's youngest daughter and that Micah was his eldest son. In my father's twisted world, I guess in some way that gave us an advantage over his other children. When he was looking to get high, he'd come looking for either my mother or Micah's.

Micah and I went to our father's funeral out of obligation more than respect. He floated in and out of our lives – in when he wanted sex or drugs from our mothers, out when he was getting them from his other women. I barely spoke to my father and knew little about him. What I did know was that he had several drugs of choice — alcohol, crack, pills — but heroin was his favorite. My strongest memories of him involved he and my mother hunched over on our living room couch, eyelids low with drool dripping from their lips. I also saw him several times on 8th Avenue doing what I call the *dope fiend lean.* I'd look at the ground, avoiding eye contact and pretending not to know him.

I also knew that my father slept with anyone who would give him a place to stay for the night. I always assumed he had other children. Micah was the only one I'd ever met. We'd been close ever since the funeral.

I had no luck getting through to Micah's place or his cell. Both lines were out of service. I figured he didn't pay his bill. I decided to go over to his place anyway.

Like bees in a hive, there were always people coming in and out of Micah's building. I didn't need to be buzzed in. I climbed four flights of stairs, took a couple of seconds to catch my breath, and pounded on the door. I kept knocking until I heard a voice.

"Who is it?"

"Micah, open up. It's Gia. My mom's trippin' again and stole my money and–"

A large Puerto Rican man with sweat stains underneath the arms of his T-shirt opened the door.

"Can I help you?"

"Yeah. Where the hell is Micah?" I asked with one hand on my hip and the other holding up my bag.

"Oh, you mean the guy who lived here before me?"

"What do you mean 'lived here before'? Did he move or something?"

"I'm sorry. Who are you?"

"Who are you, and where's my brother?" I shifted my weight.

"Yeah, he moved. He moved to a much bigger house. He's in jail."

"What?" I felt my knees get weak. I sat on the floor and hung my head between my knees. I didn't want to believe that my brother was in jail. He was a good guy. He's wasn't perfect, but he wasn't bad either. He was my big brother.

"You all right?" the man asked, still standing in the doorway.

"I'm fine. Where's the nearest police station?"

"A couple of blocks from here."

"Thanks." I grabbed my bags and made my way out.

"Hey, it's getting dark. I know I'm not your brother, but you can still spend the night," the man said as I walked away. I didn't care how dark it was getting or how late it was. I'd be damned if I was going to stay with some perverted stranger.

I found out my brother was in a jail in Westchester County for drug possession. I planned on taking the trip to Westchester in the morning. I had $100 to my name and would need at least twenty of it to get to Westchester and back. That left me with little money to find a place to spend the night.

4

A TEMPORARY HOME

I found a cheap motel on the Grand Concourse that charged by the hour. It wasn't the Waldorf Astoria, but it had a bed, a shower, and a lock on the door, which was all I needed.

The lobby stunk of booze and cheap perfume. It was cluttered with fake, dusty, plastic plants. Paper Valentine's Day hearts plastered the walls and hung from the ceiling. A fat man who looked as if he hadn't showered in days sat behind the counter, watching a small black-and-white television. His arms were crossed and rested on his potbelly.

"Can I get a room?" I asked.

He reached for his cigar, took a pull, and blew the smoke into my face. I waved my hand in front of my face and coughed directly in his.

"How long you staying?" he asked with his eyes glued to the television.

"Till eight tomorrow morning."

"You stay a second more, you pay."

I rolled my eyes, slammed the money on the counter, and snatched the key out of his hand.

Room 511. The pay-by-the-hour motels never had elevators, so I had to drag my stuff up five flights of stairs. On the way up, I passed a woman with a long, matted wig the color of chocolate milk. Bright red lipstick was smeared all over the edges of her lips. She stuffed money inside of her bra, curled up the corner of her lips, and sucked her teeth as she passed me. I looked her up and down, smirked, and continued up the stairs.

When I finally got to the fifth floor, I wanted to turn around and go back downstairs. There were three men at the end of the hallway sitting on a radiator. One was tying a brown leather belt around his arm, and the other was hunched over lifelessly the way my mother and father did on my living room couch when I was a child.

I tried to open the door, but something was wrong with the key. I fidgeted with it, glancing back at the men down the hall.

"Hey, little ma. You need help?" one of them slurred. I kicked the door and tried to push the key in further.

"Damn it," I whispered, as the man got up and moved toward me. My heart pounded against the walls of my chest harder than I pounded on the door. I twisted the knob forcefully, and the door finally opened. I ran inside and bolted the door. I looked through the peephole and saw the man standing there. He pummeled the door. I jumped backed and tripped over a small coffee table.

"I'm calling security!"

"This motel ain't got no damn security," he laughed.

"Well, then I'm calling the cops!" The banging stopped, and I took a deep breath.

The paint on the walls was peeling. The room was carpeted with the same ugly, red carpet as the lobby, and it smelled of mold. The green flowers on the bedspread matched the ones on the curtains. The tiles in the bathroom were stained brown, and the faucet leaked. I took a couple of towels and laid them over the bedsheets and pillow to prevent catching whatever might have been dwelling there. The bulb of the light on the nightstand blew when I attempted to turn it on. I opened the curtains. A neon green sign advertising live peep shows illuminated the room. I took out my headphones and lay on top of the towels.

I placed my hands behind my head and closed my eyes. I tried to block out the events of the day. I was no longer in a seedy motel on the Grand Concourse; I was back in my dorm room. I wasn't lying on prophylactic towels; I was lying on clean bedsheets. The men in the hallway shooting up were replaced by rowdy freshman who were quickly quieted by the R.A. All was silent, and I slept soundly.

5

FINDING BIG BROTHER

I woke up at seven the next morning to call Gladys to explain all that was happening with my mother and brother. She told me I could take the entire week off if I needed to. I told her I only needed a day.

I walked into the police station's narrow entrance and put my belongings on a conveyer belt that led to an X-ray machine. I walked through the metal detector without a buzz. As I walked to the end of the conveyer belt to get my things, I heard one of the security guards whisper to another, "Man, I was hoping I'd have to frisk her." The other snickered and undressed me with his eyes. My clenched teeth caged various four-letter words that were dying to escape. Seeing Micah was my only priority. I swallowed the unspoken obscenities, along with my pride, and kept it moving.

The room was crowded like a barber shop on a Friday night. To my left stood a woman holding a baby in her arms. The baby rested its head on the silk ruffles that flowed down the front of her blouse like rich vanilla icing on an expensive wedding cake. The baby's legs were wrapped around the waist of the woman's D&G tailored skinny jeans. The gold charms that adorned her open-toed stilettos looked more expensive than any piece of jewelry I owned. A Coach bag swung around the wrist of her other arm. The leather wasn't stiff and shiny like the fake Canal Street bags. It looked smoother than her baby's skin. I was no expert when it came to designer names. But when you live in New York long enough, you learn to spot a fake Canal Street special a mile away. It was the total ensemble of the person holding the bag that gave away its authenticity.

Her hair was straight with big, bouncy curls at the ends that flowed past her shoulders. Modest diamond studs sparkled from her earlobes. A diamond ring the size of a marble weighed down her right ring finger. The bangles that hung from her wrist were white gold and complemented the ring perfectly. She was well put together from head to toe.

An officer came into the room and started to run down a list of rules that most people in the room, including me, ignored. As he babbled, the woman looked down, slipped the ring off her right hand, and placed it on her left.

I'd seen her type before. Everything she wore was paid for with her man's drug money. She played the part when she came to visit. When he got back home, he'd find out through the neighborhood grapevine that she was sleeping with several of his homeboys, and it would be over. She'd still walk away with the ring, her wardrobe, and the baby, who was the most valuable commodity.

My focus shifted when a group of men walked through the door. I smiled the second I saw him. An inch was all there was between his head and the frame of the door. If his shoulders and back were any wider, he would've had to enter sideways. His dark skin was a beautiful, a striking contrast to his white teeth.

"Hey, Mich." I hugged him.

"Hey, Gia. I'm real surprised to see you. You just get back from school?" He was beaming at seeing me, and I felt warm all over.

"Yeah. I tried calling you while I was away and I went to your old apartment. Micah, what happened?"

"I got caught up, Gia. Don't worry about all that. I'm aight. But, how are you? How was your first semester?" He playfully hit me in the arm.

"It went well. They don't play up there. You can tell most of the people there had no type of freedom when they were living at home. They're wild. Smitts would make a killing up there."

Micah laughed and nodded. Smitts was a well-known drug dealer around the Polo Grounds.

"I see college has taught you more than book knowledge, G." He folded his arms.

"Yeah. But, my scholarship pays for that book knowledge, so that's what I'm there for."

"I hear that, lil' sis." He smiled. "You're not messin' with any boys up there, are you?" His smile faded.

"You must not have heard me the first time, Micah. I have a full ride to an Ivy League school. The only boys I'm messing with are Freud, Maslow, Thoreau, and Sophocles."

"Yo, what kind of crazy names parents giving their kids these days? Yo, stay away from those dudes, Gia," he joked.

I laughed so hard that I started to hiccup.

"*Hiccup! A-hiccup*," he said, mocking me.

"Shut...*hicc*...up, Micah!" I took a deep breath, puffed my cheeks, and held my breath.

"You good, Gia? They gone?"

I exhaled. "I think I'm good."

"Aight, G," he laughed.

"So, when do you get out of here, Micah?"

"I don't even know, Gia. My lawyer's trying for eight years with parole."

"Eight years, Micah? What the hell did you have in that car? Every coca plant in Columbia? You do know I graduate in *four* years, right?"

"Yeah, G. I know. Don't worry. I'm working on getting outta here as soon as possible. So, when I'm gonna see you again, G?"

"I don't know. I'll try to come by in a couple days."

"Aight, so can I call you at your mother's house?"

"I'm not staying there."

"What?"

"You know crackheads can't be trusted, Micah. She stole my money the day I came home."

"So, where the hell you staying, G?" His jawbone jutted tensely.

"I stayed at a motel last night. I'll figure it out. Don't worry about me, Mich."

"I'm not feeling that, G."

"If you need to contact me, call the Center. I'm working there till I go back to school."

"Yo, G. Write down this number."

I took out a pen and the receipt for my Metro-North ticket, and wrote down the number he gave me.

"This is my boy Sam's number. He's a good dude. Call him if you need a place to stay."

"Okay."

"I love you, G. Take care of yourself."

"I love you too, Mich." I reached in my back pocket, pulled out a piece of paper, and handed it to him. "Here, you can work on this for next time."

He unfolded the paper. It was a poem by Claude McKay that I copied out of my book. Micah never finished high school and barely finished middle school. Before I left for college, I was helping him with his reading so he could take his GED exam.

"I'm not sure if they still offer degrees here in jail, but I figured this might help if they did. Even if they don't, you're still taking that GED test when you get out of here."

"Thanks, G. I'm gonna read it tonight. Good looking out,

lil' sis. I love you."

"Love you too, Mich." I hugged him, glanced over his shoulder, and saw someone I recognized. His name was James, and he lived in the Polo Grounds. He sat with the woman I noticed earlier. He pointed to me and said something to her. I looked away and let go of Micah.

"I love you, Mich. I'll see you soon.

"Aight, G."

I walked to the door and felt a tap on my shoulder.

"You Gia?" she asked, getting a better grasp on her baby.

"Yeah."

"I'm Janay. Jay told me to give you a ride home. You live in the Polo Grounds, right?"

"Jay?"

"Yeah. My fiancé." She pointed to James. "He said you two known each other since you were kids and that you're like cousins. You need a ride?"

"I'm good. I can get on the Metro-North."

"Nah, girl. Come on. It's not a problem. I can give you a ride. He said not to let you say no."

I must have spoken to James a total of three times in my eighteen years of living in the Polo Grounds. The first time was when I was fifteen and he was twenty-one. The second time was about a year later when he must have thought age sixteen made me legal. The third time was right before I left for school.

James was like a weed in a garden. He looked harmless and even good at times. But if you didn't cut him down quick enough, he'd destroy and suck the life out of all the beautiful flowers around him.

It was freezing outside, and it would take me three times as long to get home if I took public transportation, so I gave in.

"Okay, I'll take the ride. Thanks." I expected that James would eventually ask me for something in return for this favor. I didn't intend to repay.

We walked outside, and Janay pulled out her car keys. She disabled the alarm and unlocked the doors from her keychain. The headlights lit up on a light blue Mercedes Benz convertible that was parked in a handicapped spot.

I was hoping it'd be a quiet car ride, but I was wrong. The music blasted while the baby slept in a car seat in the back. Janay sped down the highway, read and sent texts on her phone, and tried to talk to me above the music all at the same time.

"So, you and Jay tight?" she asked.

I lied. If I went against James's word, there was no telling what Janay would do. "Yeah, we grew up together. We're practically family. How long you been with him?"

"Two years. We're getting married in April."

She took her left hand off the steering wheel to show me her engagement ring. I thought back to the brief conversation I had with James a couple of days before I left for school. I also remembered the girls I'd seen him with over the last two years.

"I've never seen you before. You live uptown?"

"Nah, I live in Jersey. Jay and I met at Platinum."

Platinum was a club downtown. I wasn't into clubs. And if I was, Platinum would not be the one I would choose. Going to Platinum was just as bad as going to a house party in the projects.

"Oh, okay. Well, congrats on the wedding." I looked at the trees speeding past us on the Sprain Brook Parkway.

"Yeah, girl. It's crazy. I'm excited, but busy as hell." She popped her gum.

"Yeah, I can imagine." I had no desire to finish the conversation. I had nothing in common with this girl and actually felt sorry for her. She kept on talking.

"So, what do you do?"

"I'm in school. I'm just back home for Christmas break."

"Oh. Where you go?"

"Brown University. It's in Rhode Island."

"That's cool." I thanked God for small miracles when her

phone started buzzing. "Hello? Hey, what's up?" She lowered her voice.

I assumed it was one of her other men. I stared out the window and contemplated where I was going to spend the night. I decided to have Janay drop me off at the Polo Grounds. From there, I'd hop on the train and go to the Center.

We were back in Harlem by noon. "Thanks for the ride. Next time you see James, tell him I said thanks."

"Okay." She reached into her wallet and pulled out $100 bill. "James told me to give you this and that he'll see you around when he comes back home."

I wasn't as surprised by the money as I was by this girl's ignorance. I looked at the baby sleeping in the back. She was beautiful.

"Keep it. Tell him I said thanks and that I'll see him soon."

I shut the door. Janay sped off and made a sharp U-turn, merging onto the FDR Drive. I considered going upstairs to my mother's apartment but decided against it. I couldn't risk her stealing the small amount of money I had left. Instead, I got on the D-train and headed down to the Center.

I stayed with Gladys the next couple of days. We'd go to work together in the mornings and leave the Center together in the evenings. She even offered to let me stay at her place while the Center was closed for Christmas break. I gave her $20 from every paycheck to help offset some of the cost of me staying with her.

Everything was okay until the week before Christmas. It was about six thirty PM. All the kids were gone for the day, and I was cleaning up. The doorbell rang. I looked up and saw who it was through the small glass window of the door. My hands shook, and my Windex and paper towels fell to the floor. A knot formed in my stomach, and I felt like all the color had drained from my face. I stood frozen, unable to move. The doorbell rang a second time, and my heart raced. I stared at the man waiting at the door.

6

AN UNWELCOMED VISITOR

"**G**ia, girl. What's wrong with you?" Gladys asked. "Can't you hear that doorbell ringing?"

I picked up the paper towels and Windex. Gladys pressed the intercom button and asked, "Can I help you?"

"I'm here to see Gia." He smiled and waved at me.

Gladys looked at me. "Well, Gia, you know this guy?"

"Let him in, Gladys," I said reluctantly, placing the cleaning supplies on the table next to me.

"Hi, I'm Stephen." He shook Gladys's hand. "I'm a friend of Gia's."

"Well, any friend of Gia's is a friend of mine. Come on in." She placed her hand on the back of his shoulder and escorted him inside. If the room were pitch black, his smile could have lit it up. He practically ran to me with his arms extended.

"Gia." He said my name as if he were exhaling it.

I'd never been more physically attracted to anyone. His eyelashes were long and curled, protecting his beautiful eyes like they knew the significance of their job. His skin was the color of autumn, a mix of deep earth tones that were exciting to look at.

He was dressed as if he just walked out of a Gap ad. He wore dark blue jeans and a gray cashmere sweater. His vintage Chuck Taylors matched the red, collared shirt he wore underneath his sweater.

My arms lay limp at my sides while he hugged me. I stared over his shoulder at nothing in particular.

I'd declined a scholarship to Columbia, the closest good school, for a reason. I wanted to keep my home life and school life completely separate. And now, with Stephen standing there, that was all slipping through my fingers.

"What are you doing here, Stephen?" I stepped away from him.

"Well, don't sound so excited to see me." He forced a laugh. Then, finally responding to the expression on my face, he stepped back. "Sorry, Gia. I didn't mean to upset you." His smile faded.

"Stephen, I–" I sighed, searching for the right words to say. They weren't there. Instead, thoughts of my crack-addicted mother, my imprisoned brother, and the duffel bag I was living out of inundated my mind.

Stephen had grown up in an upper middle-class suburb outside of Boston. His mother was a lawyer, his father was a professor, and he was an only child. Explaining my situation to Stephen was futile. He couldn't begin to understand it all.

"Gia, is everything all right?" Gladys asked.

"Yeah, Gladys. I'm fine. Listen, Stephen, I really have to get back to work, so if you wouldn't mind–" I picked the cleaning supplies back up.

"Oh. Well, what time do you get off?"

"In about a half hour," I said, looking at my watch.

"I can wait. Is there anywhere I can grab a snack?"

"Just hold on. Let me finish washing these windows." I felt my cheeks getting warm. I felt Stephen's eyes watching me do something his family probably paid someone to do.

✱✱

Stephen wanted to eat at Sylvia's, a well-known soul food restaurant in Harlem. He said it was one of his parents' favorite restaurants in the city and that he had to try it out. I'd never been to Sylvia's, and now my first time there was going to be with a preppy suburbanite.

Stephen followed the waitress, and I followed Stephen. I plodded through the restaurant and was shocked to see that the majority of people eating there were white tourists. No one paid any attention to Stephen and me.

"Gia," he said as we sat down, "You've been really quiet. Is everything okay?"

I hadn't spoken more than two words since we left the Center.

"Um," I hesitated.

I looked straight into his eyes for the first time that night. They were wide and attentive. I looked away. It didn't bother me that Stephen would never understand where I came from. It bothered me that he showed up unannounced, forcing me to share details of my life that I wasn't ready to.

"Do you know what you're going to eat?" I looked at the menu, avoiding his eyes.

"Gia! I came here all the way from Boston. You've spoken less than ten words to me since I got here, and all you can say is, 'Do I know what I want to eat?'" He slid his chair closer to the table and threw his napkin into his lap.

"Stephen, I didn't invite you here. How the hell did you find me anyway? I never told you where I lived. And what makes you think you can just come here and expect me to drop everything and give you my undivided attention? "

At least, I didn't think I did. I really was happy to see him but was so unsure of how he'd feel after he learned about my crazy home life.

"Gia, I'm sorry. I assumed–"

"You know what they say about people who assume, Stephen. They make an ass–"

"Are you ready to order?" asked the waitress, tapping her pen against a small notepad.

"Not yet. Can you come back in a couple of minutes?" Stephen asked.

"No problem." She walked away.

"Maybe I shouldn't have just popped up on you like this. But my church is doing some volunteer work in Brooklyn. The thought of being so close and not seeing you drove me crazy. I just had to see you."

"Excuse me, Stephen." I pushed away from the table and walked to the door. I heard him calling my name but I kept walking.

I walked up 126th and turned right on Madison so that Stephen couldn't catch up to me on Lenox.

I shoved my hands into my coat pockets and looked down, avoiding the wind. I hummed the melody to Robin Thicke's *Complicated*.

When I reached the intersection of 124th and Madison, I remembered that, unlike the pedestrian walk signal, I didn't want to change. I stopped humming the lyrics of the song.

The couch in Gladys's living room seemed unusually lumpy that night. I felt like the princess in *The Princess and the Pea*. No matter how I twisted or turned, I just couldn't fall asleep.

It was typical for Gladys or her boyfriend to pass through the living room to go into the kitchen and get a drink or a snack. But something was different that night.

Gladys's boyfriend got up to get water several times. The

floorboards whined under the weight of his feet, letting me know he was pacing. I felt him watching me, though my eyes were closed. I tried not to move, hoping he'd go back to his room.

I heard him come closer and smelled his acrid breath. It labored as it spread across the side of my cheek. I opened my eyes, jumped back, and pulled the blanket up to my neck. He leaned in, pushed the hair away from my face, and tried to pull the blanket down. I stood up and staggered backward but stopped when I bumped into the entertainment center behind me. He cornered me, shoving his hand up the leg of my shorts.

"Who you think Gladys is gonna believe, Gia?" he whispered. "If you're smart, you'll just lie back down and let nature take its course."

He pushed me on the couch and slid his hand up my shirt.

"Where you gonna stay if she kicks you out? Huh, Gia? You gonna lay this warm, pretty little body down in the cold hard streets of Harlem?"

He kissed my neck. I wasn't sure that Gladys would take my word over his, but I decided to chance it.

"Take your filthy hands off of me," I said through my teeth. I spit on him and he laughed.

"Gia, you must've known I like a challenge."

He placed one hand over my mouth and used the other to rip my shorts. The horrible thought of losing my virginity to a rapist fueled me.

I bit his hand so hard that it started to bleed. I spat, not wanting any of his fluid in my mouth. He snatched it back and attempted to shake away the pain. He looked down at his bloody hand.

"Bitch!" he yelled, raising his other hand to strike me. Without looking, I grabbed a vase from the entertainment center behind me.

"*Uh!*" I smashed the vase over his head. He crumpled to the floor along with the shards of glass from the broken vase. He moaned and rolled around. I looked up when I saw the hallway light come on.

Gladys stood there unfazed. She made her way into the kitchen and got a tray of ice, a dishrag, and a roll of paper towels. She kneeled near his head, wrapped the ice in the dishrag, and held it against his forehead. She wadded the paper towels with her other hand and pressed them against his bleeding hand. She looked up at me. I looked away. She shifted off her knees and sat next to him, lifting his head off the floor and into her lap. I grabbed my bag, went into the bathroom, changed my clothes, and left.

7

STAYING WITH SAM

It was three AM. The steam coming from my mouth made it to the payphone before I did. I took my hands out of my coat pockets and rubbed them together like they were two sticks trying to ignite a fire. I pulled out a piece of paper from my purse, wiped the earpiece of the phone with the sleeve of my coat, and dialed the number.

"Hello?" A raspy voice answered.

"Is this Sam?"

"Yeah. Who this?"

"This is Gia. Sorry to wake you. My brother Micah gave me your number."

"What up, Gia?" His voice was much clearer now. "Where you at? You okay?"

"Uh, well, my brother said if I needed a place to stay–"

"Where you at? I'll come get you." I heard a bed squeak in the background.

"Well, I'm near 116th and Lenox. I can get on the train. What train do you live by?"

"Nah, don't move. I'll be there in five minutes."

"But–" I heard a dial tone. I looked at the phone as if it

offended me and hung it up. Had Micah already told him I might call? I clutched my bag and looked around nervously. I'd never met Sam and kept reminding myself that, if he was a friend of Micah's, I should trust him.

I heard someone call my name five minutes later.

"Ay yo, Gia," a man screamed from down the block.

My eyes widened. Sam looked like a linebacker rushing the quarterback. My instinct was to step back. His sweats hugged his massive thighs. His arms barely hit the sides of his body.

He grabbed the bag off my shoulder and started walking.

"What you doing outside by yourself at three in the morning? Yo, if Mich knew you were outside all crazy like this, he'd be tight." He shook his head.

"Yeah, I know. Thanks for–"

"Don't even go there, G." He turned and looked at me. "Mich is like my brother, so that makes you my sister." He turned back around and continued walking. "You can stay with me as long as you want, under one condition."

I stopped walking and looked back at the train station. I knew there'd be a catch. He turned back around.

"You are *not* allowed to thank me. My place is your place. I live right around the block. You can stay with me as long as you need to."

"Thanks. I mean, all right, Sam." I didn't even bother making promises of when I'd leave. The only thing I was sure of was that I was going back to school the weekend before Martin Luther King Day, which was a little under a month away. I didn't plan on inconveniencing Sam for that long.

"My girl's upstairs sleeping. She don't pay the bills, so she ain't got nothing to say. You stay as long as you want, and make yourself at home." He unlocked the door to his building.

The lobby reeked of Pine-Sol. It was much better than

urine and cigarettes. The building was no frills, but it wasn't the projects. The halls were well lit. The floor tiles were polished and not cracked. The paint on the walls was smooth.

We rode the elevator to the sixth floor. The apartment was nice. The furniture was contemporary and in good condition. I looked down and saw my silhouette reflected in the hardwood floors.

"Watch whatever you want whenever you want." Sam noticed my reaction to his plasma television and extensive DVD library.

"Thanks." I said, sitting on the couch. I ran my hand across the leather, hoping my body wouldn't stick to it while I slept.

"Na, G. You don't gotta sleep on the couch. I got an extra room. Follow me."

I followed Sam down the hall. My room was the first door on the right.

"Make yourself comfortable." He put my bag next to the bed.

"Sam–"

He interrupted me. "Remember our condition, Gia."

"Right." I sat on the bed.

"Okay, cool. Your bathroom is right across the hall. Me and my girl have our own bathroom in our room, so this one's all yours. I get up real early for work, but I try not to make a whole lot of noise in the morning. My girl don't do a damn thing but sit up in this house all day or spend my money downtown. She keeps the house clean, and she's a hell of a cook, so she'll take good care of you. I gotta leave for work in about an hour, so you good?"

"I'm perfect. You want to come with me some time this week to go check Micah?"

"Yeah, but I need to check my work schedule. I do construction so it's kind of crazy sometimes. Let me know when you're going, and I'll let you know."

"Okay. Good night."

"Night, G."

I changed into my pajamas and got into bed. I thought about how I would get through the next few weeks. What was I going to do for money? Would I stay here until it was time to go back to school? I knew Sam wouldn't mind, but I couldn't help but think that I was inconveniencing him and his girl.

I heard Sam leave just about an hour after we got in. It was the last thing I remembered before falling asleep.

I woke up at noon to an amazing smell. I remembered what Sam said about his girlfriend being a great cook. I headed to the bathroom to shower.

Afterward, I followed the scent into the kitchen. I stood at the entrance and looked in.

"Aw, damn," she said, flipping a pancake. "See, you're lucky you're Micah's little sis because I would *never* let a woman as beautiful as you up in my house around my man." She pointed the spatula at me, smiling.

"Thanks." I took a seat at the kitchen table.

She was right about one thing. She had nothing to worry about. Sam wouldn't even dream of making a move on me if he and Micah were as close as they claimed.

"You hungry?" she asked, turning off the stove. I thought back to the last meal I had. I should have eaten at Sylvia's. I hadn't had anything to eat for almost twenty-four hours.

"Definitely. Sam told me you're an amazing cook." I pushed my chair in closer to the table.

She put bacon, eggs, and pancakes on a plate. "Yeah, I'm aight."

"Thank you." I wiped the sides of my mouth as she set the plate down, trying to prevent saliva from running down the sides of it. I didn't know if it was her cooking or my starvation, but I cleaned my plate within minutes.

"So, how long have you and Sam known each other?" I used the fork to scrape the syrup off my plate.

"Well, we've known each other since we were kids. We were high school sweeties on and off for a couple years. You know how that goes."

I didn't but nodded anyway.

"And now, here we are." She raised her hands in the air.

"Oh, okay. Cool. Sam seems like a good guy. My brother Micah is crazy overprotective of me so–"

"Yeah, your brother's a good dude. Him and Sam been boys since we were all in high school together. So, you in college?"

"Yeah. I go to school in Rhode Island."

"Girl, that's good. Do your thing, girl. You got a boyfriend?"

"No. Men have nothing to offer me that I can't offer myself right now." *Besides a place to lay my head and money to get me back to school,* I thought to myself.

"Good. Men ain't nothing but trouble. Keep doing you. If a good one comes along, great. If not, you're a beautiful, young, educated black woman. The sisters are doing it for themselves, and you gonna be all right," she said, snapping her fingers.

I laughed. "Thanks. I don't even know your name."

"I'm sorry, girl. I'm Debra, but everyone calls me Dee."

"Nice to meet you, Dee."

"You too, Gia. Does anyone call you anything for short?"

"Yeah, Gia," I laughed. "My brother calls me G."

"All right, well. I like Gia. So, Gia, what you trying to get into today?" She took my plate to the sink.

"Well, I need to find a job. I was working at an after-school program, but that fell through. I was thinking about going downtown to see if I could get a job at one of the stores. They usually look for extra help during the holidays don't they?"

"Girl, please. It's too late for all that. Them stores been

had people filling out applications long before the holidays. I have a friend who might be able to hook you up. But, you wouldn't be working in the stores. He's a party promoter. He throws all the hot parties all over the city. He's always looking for pretty girls to help him out."

"I don't really do the clubs."

I'd never even been inside of a club. In New York, you had to be twenty-one to get into most clubs and I was only eighteen. All I knew about the clubs was that they were meat markets filled with men who couldn't keep their hands to themselves. It wasn't my idea of a good time.

"Would you do clubs for $200 a night?"

"$200 a night?" What would I possibly be doing that would pay $200 a night? This sounded fishy already.

"His name is Ty. I'll give you his cell number, and you can give him a call. He'll give you all the details. If you think it's cool, then cool. You got a job. If you ain't with it, you can go downtown and try your luck at the stores."

"I guess," I said, thinking I had nothing to lose.

8

THE INTRODUCTION

"**Y**o, this is Ty." The voice was deep and smooth.

"Hi, Ty. My name's Gia. I got your number from Dee."

"Harlem Dee?"

"Yeah, Harlem Dee." I assumed he knew a lot of Dees but only one from Harlem, so I agreed.

"Okay. So what's up?"

"I'm looking for work for the next couple of weeks while I'm off from school. Dee said you might be able to help me out."

"School? How old are you?"

"Eighteen."

"How old you look?"

I didn't have an answer. People always assumed I was older than I was because of the way I carried myself. If they judged by the way I dressed, they'd probably guess that I was eighteen. I kept it simple — jeans, T-shirt, and sneakers. My sneakers weren't from Payless, but they weren't Jordans either. I didn't see the point in spending an entire paycheck on a pair of sneakers. Sneakers were made for feet. Feet were made to take me from point A to B. Point A's street was usually littered with the same trash, chewed gum, dog — and sometimes even human — waste, and other unidentifiable filth as point B's. Buying an expensive pair of sneakers was like wadding up a stack of cash and throwing it into a landfill. It was a waste.

I didn't do heels because I was already five-foot-eight and didn't need the extra height. I also never really had anywhere all that nice to go. I wasn't much into bags either. What was the point of spending an insane amount of money on a bag that would leave the wallet inside of it empty? I usually slung a cheap, oversized purse around my shoulder to carry my books, wallet, Vaseline, and lotion in. I didn't wear much jewelry. My ears weren't even pierced. I always wore a watch because my time was valuable, although the watch itself wasn't worth much.

I never made up my face. My skin was clear, and I intended to keep it that way. My lips were already pink, so I wore clear lips gloss or Vaseline in the winter. My hair was usually parted on the side and tied back into a bun, out of my face and out of the way.

Even though I spent more time on my mind than my body, I got just as much attention from men as the girls who looked like it took them hours to get ready.

"Twenty-one." I gave him the answer I assumed he wanted to hear.

"You been in the clubs before?" he asked over the sound of tires speeding over wet pavement in the background.

"Yeah," I said flatly.

"Aight. Well, I gotta see what you look like. What you up to today?"

"I'll be downtown on 34th Street."

"Aight. I'll meet you in front of Macy's in an hour. Cool?"

"Okay. I'll be there." I put on my coat.

"Aight."

I didn't know what to expect, but I needed cash and I needed it fast. I needed my own place to stay, and I needed to get back to school in a couple of weeks. I also had no money for books for the next semester.

I looked in the mirror, smoothed out my eyebrows with my fingers, ran my tongue across my teeth, and smiled at my reflection. I hoped I was what Ty was looking for.

34th Street the week before Christmas. My suggestion to meet there was just plain stupid. It teemed with more tourists than Times Square. But on top of the tourists were New Yorkers. Everyone was out shopping for last-minute Christmas gifts.

The lampposts looked like candy canes. Storefronts were so beautifully decorated that people waited in line to see them. The NYPD barricades closed off 34th Street, giving pedestrians and their shopping bags free range of the street. *Have Yourself a Merry Little Christmas* crawled out of the horn of a nearby saxophone, following me from the A Train to Macy's. It lost its wind after a block and was unable to push through the revolving door behind me.

I saw a tall, light-skinned man with eyes the color of kiwis and dreadlocks that looked like live, strong vines leaning against the Clinique counter. I instinctively knew it was Ty.

"Are you Ty?" I asked, leaning against the counter beside him.

He looked up from his phone. The wooden toothpick he chewed on dropped when his jaw did, a sign that he was pleased with what he saw.

Without looking, he slid his phone into his pocket and licked his lips. He gave me a quick look up and down and nodded. He cracked a quarter of a smile. He was attractive. I extended my hand to shake his, remembering I was there for a job and not a boyfriend.

"I'm Gia," I said, tightening my grip.

"That's some handshake you got there, Gia."

"So I've been told." I let go. Strong handshake, strong woman.

"Aight, so here's the deal. You got the look, and you seem about your business, so you got the job. I own and operate my own promotion company, Sapphire Entertainment. I host the hottest urban, upscale parties in the city. I throw a party just about every day of the week. I'm gonna start you out in the front. You'll be my guest list girl. Basically, you check names off the guest list in the front, and at two AM, when the guest list closes, you go inside and make sure the VIPs are taken care of. You cool standing outside in the cold in a dress and heels?"

I hated the cold. And, I wasn't sure if I could even walk in heels let alone stand in the freezing cold in them for hours. But all that was irrelevant. I needed the cash.

"Yeah, that's cool."

"Aight, so I need you on tonight at Ice. It's on 28th and 6th. Tight black dress, heels, makeup, and hair down. You said you're nineteen, right?

"Eighteen."

"You in college?"

"Yeah."

"Where you go? City College? Hunter?"

"No. Brown. It's in Rhode Island."

"Oh, word? That's what's up." He nodded in approval. "Well, since you're a college girl, you're probably on a budget, right?"

"Yeah." That was a nice way of putting it. I was broke.

He pulled out his wallet.

"Here's $300. Go to the fourth floor and ask for Vanessa. She'll help you pick out a dress. After you get a dress, she'll point you in the direction of the shoes. In the shoe department, ask for Stacy. She'll hook you up with a fresh set of heels. Remind her they need to be open-toed in case she forgets. You said you stay in Harlem, right?"

"Yeah."

"Aight, so after you get the shoes and dress, head uptown to 121st and Lex. There's a Dominican salon on the corner. They'll hook you up with a wash, set, and blow. There should be a couple of nail shops in the area too. Get a manicure and pedicure."

He grabbed my hand and looked at my nails.

"Beautiful." He looked up from my hand into my eyes.

He held my hand for a second longer than normal. I pulled it away, and he shoved his in his pocket, cleared his throat, and continued talking. "You won't need tips. Your nails are pretty enough. Just a regular manicure is cool. Do you have makeup?"

"No, I don't." I looked at the makeup counters that surrounded us.

"Natural beauties like you never do. It's cool. Follow me."

We left the traditional Christmas music that played at the Clinique counter and followed the sounds of Mary J. Blige's *Christmas in the City* which blared from the speakers near the Mac counters. Unlike Clinique and the other makeup counters, Mac had different counters for different parts of the face. People applied lip gloss at small mirrors in one section. Others sat in director-type chairs while Mac employees applied their makeup. I followed Ty to a woman behind the eye counter. When she saw Ty, her smile grew to be bigger than the fake eyelashes she wore.

"Hey, Ty." She walked from behind the counter and gave Ty a kiss on both cheeks, the way I'd seen people do in French films.

"Niceey, this is Gia. Gia, this is Niceey." We shook hands. She smiled again, but it was different than the one she shot Ty.

"Wow, she's really pretty, Ty. And, she has amazing skin."

She inspected my face.

"Yeah, can you hook her up? Whole face and whatever colors you use on her, bag 'em up. I'll be buying them."

"Okay. Is she working the clubs?" Niceey pulled samples from the counter.

"Yeah. Dark on the eyes, but not scary, and make the lips pop."

He focused in on my lips and bit his. Uncomfortable with them talking about me like I wasn't there, I added my two cents.

"Yeah, and go easy on the foundation. I ain't trying to break out all crazy or look like a clown." I wanted to take control of the conversation.

"No problem. Have a seat." She patted the chair next to the counter. "I'll be back." She went to collect the makeup.

"Gia, you're in good hands. I'll be back in about ten minutes."

He walked off to one of the other departments. As he walked away, reality crept in. I just met this guy twenty minutes ago. He gave me $300, all so I could check some names off a list for him at a club. How did he know all these women in the store anyway? Was he sleeping with all of them? How many women before me did he do this with? And, what would happen after the party was over? Would he expect me to come home with him? I needed the money, but I was nobody's prostitute. My self-respect didn't have a price tag. I looked at Niceey. She was at one of the counters with her back toward me. I looked at the exit. I stood up and sat back down when I saw Ty coming toward me. He had a small box in his hand.

"You'll need this when you're outside."

I opened the box. It was a Diesel watch. The leather band was white as new snow. The face was encrusted with small diamonds. Suspicious, I snapped the box closed and pushed it back toward Ty.

"I don't need this. I have a watch." I looked down at the one on my wrist.

"I know you have a watch, and I like that. The watch you're wearing now tells me you're focused. You know what you want, and you get it. The watch I'm giving you says not only do you know what you want, and you'll get it, but that you'll get it by any means necessary."

How naïve did this dude think I was? I let him continue anyway.

"The watch is a gift. Everything else's part of your pay."

"Speaking of pay. How much do I get?"

"It depends on how well you do. Tonight, this is your pay — the makeup, the dress, the shoes, the hair."

"Last time I checked, dresses and shoes don't pay the bills." He gave me half a smile and I had him.

"True," he laughed. "Think of tonight as your training. You do well, you work with me every day. If you don't, you can keep everything from today and any tips you make.

"Aight, that sounds fair."

He leaned in so close that I felt his breath on the nape of my neck. I thought he was going to kiss me. Instead, he stole his breath back, inhaling deeply.

"What the hell do you think you're doing, Ty?" I recoiled and looked at him.

"Chill. It ain't like that, Gia. I'll be right back." He left as Niceey came back with her arsenal of cosmetics.

"Ty is cool peoples. You're in good hands," she said, dipping a brush into a powder that matched my complexion.

"Yeah."

I wanted to keep my conversation with Niceey to a minimum. I regretted letting my guard down so easily over the last twenty minutes. I decided it was time for it to go back up.

Ty came back with a small bag.

"Spray it twice on your left wrist and rub both wrists together. Spray it once on the left side of your neck. Take your right wrist and rub it against the left side of your neck and then on the right. One small spray on your chest, and you're straight."

I looked inside the bag and saw Calvin Klein Euphoria. I had no idea what it smelled like, but assumed Ty picked it based on the smell of my neck.

"Okay." I threw the bag in my lap.

"I'll see you at Ice at ten thirty tonight. Niceey, you coming through tonight?"

"I'll try to make it if I'm not too tired after work."

I could tell she was blushing even though her skin was dark. Niceey was sprung.

"Aight. Well, if you do make it out, just see Gia at the door. She'll let you in."

"Cool." She smiled and continued putting on my makeup.

"The number you called me from earlier, is that your cell?"

"No. I don't have a cell." I must've been the only person left on the face of the planet without a cellphone.

"Aight, I'll have one for you tonight at Ice. Aight, I'm out." He pulled his phone back out of his pocket and scrolled through it as he walked away.

∗∗

The smell of Dee's cooking greeted me at the front door of Sam's apartment. I dropped my bags on the couch and followed it into the kitchen. Dee sat at the kitchen table. A small tag that read Lipton's apple cinnamon tea hung from the side of a mug that advertised tax services. She took a quick sip, placed the mug on the table, and smiled.

"What's good, girl? I see you got your hair did," she joked. I touched my hair. It'd been a while since I'd had a nice Dominican wash and set.

"Yeah." I wore my hair in a bun so often that I forgot how long it was. It was past my shoulders.

"It looks good, girl. Real good. It's so shiny." She got up and touched it. "Damn, and it's mad soft too. You must got that Injian in your family."

I laughed and said, "Injian, huh? Not Indian but Injian." We cracked up.

"So, it looks like you met Ty." She stirred something in a pot.

"Yeah. I'm working for him tonight," I answered, grabbing a bottle of water out of the refrigerator.

"Cool. He's good peoples. What's in the bags?" She looked over my shoulder at the couch.

"Just some stuff I'm wearing tonight." I walked to the living room.

"Some stuff? Damn. Ty hooked you up, huh? Can I see?"

She grabbed the bags and started going through them. She pulled out the dress first. It was black, as Ty requested. Vanessa in the dress department took one look at my body and started pulling a bunch of black dresses off the racks. But in true Gia form, I made the final decision. I might not have dressed like I walked off the runway every day, but I was no dummy. I knew what was hot and what wasn't.

The one I chose was a black pencil dress. It clung to my body like a magnet to metal. It looked like lingerie but wasn't slutty or over-the-top. It was sexy and classy. The top half of the dress looked like a corset. The straps were slightly thicker than spaghetti. The trim was lace and rested on top of my cleavage beautifully. It cinched at the waist like a rubber band around a stack of cash and tightly hugged my thighs. I felt sexy in it. Judging from the look on her face, Dee approved.

"Damn, girl. You're not playing with this dress, huh?" She ran her fingers over the smooth material.

"When it comes to money, I don't play," I said, folding the dress and placing it back in the bag.

She pulled out the shoes. Against Ty's recommendation, I didn't go to the shoe department at Macy's. I went down the street to Aldo and picked a pair of peep-toe stilettos. They were a sparkly gold and silver in a smooth, zigzag pattern. The heel looked like a gold chain and was four inches high. They made me six feet tall. To my surprise, I liked the extra height. But I was nervous about walking and standing in them for hours.

I also picked out a pair of silver earrings. I was surprised to find clip-ons. I guess I wasn't the only person left in the city who didn't have her ears pierced. They were simple, square-shaped, clunky earrings that sat heavy on my earlobes. I decided against a necklace. I didn't want any attention taken away from the lace bodice of the dress.

"Who the hell knew that the little college girl could put it together like that? What! Let me find out." Dee snapped her fingers. I smirked. "Which club you working tonight? Ice?"

"Yeah, I need to be there at ten thirty" I looked down at my watch. It was already eight.

"Aight, cool. So, we out by ten?" Dee asked.

I didn't think she planned on coming with me, but I guessed it was cool. I assumed she had been to Ty's parties before. She was the one who gave me his number, and I was the one controlling the door.

"Nine forty-five."

"Okay, cool." Dee went back into the kitchen.

I looked at my new things and took a deep breath. If I got through my first semester of college, I could get through this. I collected my things and headed for my room.

9

NIGHTLIFE

Dee and I arrived at Ice at ten fifteen. The timing was perfect. I didn't get there too early, so I didn't seem overly eager. I wasn't late, which meant I took the job seriously. My motto was that, if you're on time, you're already ten minutes late. So I was five minutes early by my standard.

The club didn't look like much from the outside. If it weren't for Dee, I probably would have passed it completely. Ice was written in small, neon-blue letters on a black awning that hung over a tall, black door with a long metal handlebar. Opaque white windows as tall as the door lined the face of the building. A barrel-chested man who resembled a beast more than a human guarded the front door.

"Hey, I'm Gia. Where's Ty?" I looked up into the man's eyes. He took out a walkie-talkie and mumbled something into it.

"Follow me," he said, leading us inside.

The same neon blue that lit the sign outside dimly lit the inside of the club. A fully stocked bar sat to my immediate left. We walked down a wide isle that I later discovered was the dance floor. It extended the length of the club and terminated at another fully stocked bar.

On adjacent sides of the dance floor were platforms that were elevated just enough to put the V and I in VIP but low enough that, when the party really started, the VIPs could easily join the rest of the crowd on the dance floor. Both platforms held five separate VIP areas each. Each area consisted of a small, black, square table with a mirror glass top. Each table was surrounded by ivory-colored leather couches the color of French Vanilla ice cream. By the end of the night, they'd look more like melted rainbow sherbet consisting of blue Hawaiian, apple martini green, and Heineken gold.

The balcony held the DJ booth. A small waterfall was in the back of it. On both sides of the booth were two small rooms, the outside walls of which had the same mirror glass as the tabletops. They looked like ice cubes.

Ty sat at the bar in the back of the club.

"I got it from here. Thanks," I said to the bouncer and walked over to Ty. I tapped him on the shoulder, "So, boss, am I acceptable?" I did a three sixty. He gave me a full smile.

"You look good, G. Real good." He took a sip of his drink.

"Um hum," Dee cleared her throat. "Do I get some kind of commission for bringing her to you, Ty? You know how many dudes are gonna keep coming back to see this chick?" She sat on the stool next to Ty.

I had a hard time believing that. Would men actually come back to the club for a pretty guest list girl? I'd soon find out that Dee wasn't joking.

"Aight, sit down. I got your commission," he said to Dee. I sat on the other side of Ty.

"Thug passion for Dee and–" he paused, looked at me, and asked, "Gia, what you drinking?"

"I'll take a horse's neck," I said nonchalantly. The bartender busted out laughing. Ty and Dee followed suit.

"What the hell is a horse's neck?" Dee asked, laughing.

"That some kind of Rhode Island drink? I swear you college kids are wild with your drinking."

"She just ordered a gingerale," the bartender said, still laughing.

"Gia, don't tell me you don't drink?" Ty asked.

"Yeah, I drink. I just don't drink alcohol."

More laughs. I couldn't care less what they thought. The only difference between the alcohol they were drinking and the crack my mother smoked was that alcohol was legal and crack wasn't. Both made people do and say unbelievable things, and both were addicting. I didn't want any kind of substance to control me. I needed to be in control at all times. People taking advantage, and walking all over me was an everyday battle in this city, and I planned on continuing to win it. With drugs, it was a losing battle, and last I checked, alcohol was a drug.

"Well, we're gonna have to change all that, G. You work in a nightclub now. That's like a doctor saying he don't like blood."

This time, he sipped his drink from the straw and stared dead into my eyes. My not drinking intrigued him even more.

"Nah, she's a good college girl," Dee said. "Give her the horse's ass she asked for." We all looked at her and laughed.

I jumped when the music started playing and looked down at my watch. ten forty-five PM.

"Aight, college girl. You ready? Doors open in thirty minutes." Ty stirred his drink.

"I thought they opened at eleven?" I looked back down at my watch.

"Damn, you really never been to a club before, have you?" He shook his head.

"I told you I have." Again, I was lying. "I've just never been at a club this *early*."

"Aight. Well, doors do open at eleven. Usually around ten

thirty all the broke-ass men and women who don't want to pay a cover start lining up. But, in order to get the guys with the money to not just drive by, but actually park they whips and come inside, you gotta build up a line of pretty women outside. It's your job to stand out there and come back inside every once in a while to act like you're doing something important, while the bouncer is holding up the line. It's also your job to go out in the street, and when the dudes in the Benzes, Suburbans, and Chargers pull up and ask if it's packed inside, you lie and say it is. Ask them what bottle they want, and go put it on ice at their VIP table. Got it?"

"Got it." I got up. I walked toward the front windows that were opaque from the outside but had a clear view of the street from the inside. As Ty said, there were about ten women in line and two men. I walked back over to the bar.

"Hey, Ty. Where's my list?"

"Go see the cashier in the front. She has it. Oh, before I forget." He reached into his pocket and pulled out a cell phone. "This is yours. You can use it to contact me any time of the day or night. And I'll call it when I'm trying to get in contact with you. Don't worry about the bill. It's covered."

"Aight."

I went to the cashier's booth, which was located in the foyer at the entrance of the club. I got the guest list and clipboard and headed outside.

I looked at my watch. It was eleven. I made small talk with the bouncer, went inside, checked my makeup, talked to Dee — who was already on her third drink — and headed back outside at eleven fifteen.

"Ya'll on a list?" I asked the girls at the front of the line.

"Yeah, we on the parties.com list," one of them answered.

Sounded good enough to me. I looked them up and down. They were dressed all right enough. I looked at Brock, the bouncer. He nodded.

"Aight. How many you got with you?" I asked the girl in the front.

"Three," she answered.

I gave them three comp cards. Brock had already checked their IDs while I was inside BS-ing. If being in control was part of the job description, I was doing a damn good job. I felt comfortable in my dress and in my skin. Walking in heels came naturally. I loved the way the extra height caused me to tower over people.

By two AM, the club was packed, and the line was around the block.

"Aight, Brock. It's two. Guest list is closed. I'm heading inside."

"Aight, G."

I walked inside feeling good. I was finally out of the cold and already made $100 in tips, mostly from men who were underdressed. I wanted to keep the crowd looking good, so I didn't let men with tore-up sneakers or athletic gear in, no matter how much they offered. But, if their sneakers were clean and new, an extra $20, $40, or $50 would get them past Brock. I didn't even have to ask for the money. After seeing the line of pretty women, they were so anxious to get inside that, not only did they give me cash, but they also bought a bottle. I booked four empty VIP tables that way. I gave half the cash I made to Brock, but still came off with $50 and a handful of business cards from men who asked me out. I threw all of them in the trash.

Ty greeted me at the door when I got inside.

"Damn, G. You are doing it out there. All the VIP tables are full. You into sports?"

"No. Why? Knicks tickets part of the benefits of this job?" I pushed my hair behind my ear.

"No. You remember that group of dudes that I escorted in about a half hour ago?"

"Yeah. The big dudes?" I asked.

I remembered Ty coming outside on his phone and opening the back door of a black Escalade. Three guys who looked like linebackers stepped out and walked through with Ty.

"Yeah well *those big dudes*, as you call them, play for the Jets. And one of them is checking for you."

Checking for me? How did they even notice me? I didn't check their names off the list. Brock didn't even check their IDs. They were outside for less than two seconds.

"Okay, *and?*" I crossed my arms in front of my chest. "Am I supposed to drop my panties now or later?" I asked, rolling my eyes. "Just because they're football players, they think I'm gonna stroll up to VIP, bat my eyelashes, and it's gonna be on? I don't know what kind of girl you think I am Ty, but–"

"Whoa, G. You're so defensive all the damn time. People aren't always trying to play you. Did you ever think for one second that someone might actually, genuinely like you and want to get to know you?"

I uncrossed my arms and thought it was possible, but not all that probable. They didn't know anything about me. All they knew was what they saw, which was a small part of who I was. But, it *was* my job to check on the VIPs, even if they were cocky football players who got knocked in the head one too many times.

"Which one are they in?" I asked reluctantly.

"To the left of the DJ booth."

I paused and looked into Ty's eyes. They were no longer the sparkling green they were earlier in the day. They now looked like dull, shriveled, green olives inside a dirty martini. I turned to the balcony and made my way up the stairs. I was not prepared for what I was about to see.

The bouncer in front of the VIP room opened the door and let me in. Before I saw anything, I heard a deep voice yell something to the bouncer. Whatever he said made the bouncer shove me into the room and close the door behind me. I looked up and saw Dee with her face against the glass tabletop. She was snorting cocaine. Instinctively, I yelled for her.

"Dee! Are you serious right now?" I screamed over the music.

She lifted her head and looked at me. The person staring back at me was not the same Dee I came with. Her pupils looked like poppy seeds, and her smile was cold and vacant.

"It's aight, G. It's cool." She struggled not to laugh.

I turned around and headed for the door. Someone stopped me. It was one of the men who stepped out of the Escalade earlier in the night.

"You mind if I join you? This really ain't my kind of party either." He motioned for the door.

"Yeah." I walked out. We went downstairs to the bar.

"I'm Terrance," he shouted over the music.

"Gia. Nice to meet you," I screamed back.

"What you drinking, Gia?"

"Just water."

"That's it?"

"Yeah, that's it," I said, annoyed. I prepared to defend myself and explain once again that I didn't drink, but I didn't have to. He made his way to the bar. I followed him. I wanted to make sure he didn't try any funny business with my drink.

I wasn't the only one following him. A flock of women in tight, revealing clothes and slutty stiletto heels congregated around him at the bar. He flashed them a quick smile, ordered our drinks, and pushed through them to make his way back to me.

"Here you go." He handed me a bottled water.

"Thanks." I opened the bottle and took a drink.

"I know the music is loud, and you don't seem like the type of woman who wants some stranger you just met trying to scream in your ears over the music."

I shook my head. He was right. But I was afraid he was going to ask me to leave with him.

"Your Ty's peoples, right?"

I nodded.

"Aight. Well, I know how to get in touch with Ty. If it's cool with you, I'll get your number from him. Let him know it's cool to give it to me if it's cool with you. Ty's a good dude. He won't give me the number unless you say it's all right."

"Okay."

"I need you to do me one more quick favor. I'm about to get out of here. Can you grab my hand and walk me to the door? You ain't even gotta go outside. These women are on the prowl in here, and I'm trying to get out in one piece. Don't worry about the dudes. I can handle them myself - no homo."

He smiled sincerely. He held it long enough for me to notice his perfectly straight, white teeth and deep dimples, which looked like inverted chocolate chips. I licked my lips at the thought of the chocolate, and without a word, I grabbed his hand and walked him to the front door. He gave my hand a squeeze and headed outside with Brock. I took a quick look around and saw Ty talking to the same group of women that were trying for Terrance at the bar. I walked over and pushed my way through to Ty.

"When Terrance," I paused and started over. "*If* Terrance calls, it's cool to give him my number. You can return to your hoes now." I smiled.

"You mean Tony?"

"No *Terrance*," I shouted over the music. Ty looked confused. "Terrance!" I shouted again and walked away.

For the rest of the night, I checked on the VIPs to make sure they were having a good time and spending good money. By the end of the night, I'd made $200 in tips. I wasn't sure what for. The drink orders I did take I gave to the waitress, and she was the one doing all the work, not me. But I gladly accepted the money.

We left the club at four AM. The sky was the color of cotton candy, and the sun was coming up. I hopped in a cab with Dee. The tension inside was thicker than the exhaust from neighboring cars on the West Side Highway. I didn't want to bring up what I saw Dee doing earlier in the night, but I knew I had to.

"So, Dee. Does Sam know?"

"Does Sam know what? That I don't have a stick up my ass and actually like to have a good time on the weekend?" she slurred. I wiped her spit off of my face.

I didn't care that Dee was implying that I was the one with the stick up my ass. I was more concerned with how I was supposed to act around Sam now that I knew this new information.

"What you gonna do, Gia? You gonna tell him and get us both put out on the street?"

I didn't understand how Dee's drug use would get me put out. It was Sam's place, not hers. He was the one who paid the bills, not her. He was the one who invited me to stay, not her.

"I'm not gonna say anything, but I need to let you know. Don't *ever* bring that stuff anywhere near me. Don't talk to me about it. Don't joke with me about it. I don't want to hear anything about it. You feel me?" I stared her down.

"Aight, Gia. We cool." She leaned against the window of the cab and dozed off.

We were far from cool. I thought about the possibility of having to find somewhere new to stay. I left my apartment because my crackhead mother stole my money. There was a possibility that Dee could do the same if the urge to use hit her hard enough. I decided from that night on to sleep with all my money on me and bring it everywhere I went. I figured it was safer to have it on me in the streets than left inside of an apartment with an addict.

10

BACK UPSTATE

I woke up at eight AM after sleeping three hours. It was Sunday, and I planned on getting an early start so I could go see Micah. I walked in the kitchen to get a glass of orange juice. To my surprise, Sam was sitting at the table fully dressed, drinking a cup of coffee and reading the *Daily News*. I rarely saw Sam, because he was always working.

"Good morning." I opened the refrigerator and smiled.

"Hey, G." He put down the paper. "How you been?"

"I'm good. I thought Sunday was your day off. Why you up so early?" I poured my OJ and joined him at the table.

"Well, when you get up for work at four every morning, eight AM is sleeping in. And church starts at ten."

"Church?" I wasn't expecting that. Sam was a good guy, and most of the people I knew who went to church weren't. They were in the clubs getting drunk and high on Saturday night, and repenting and praising on Sunday. The only exception was my grandmother. I went with her every Sunday until she passed. I did it mostly out of respect for her. I didn't knock people who believed in God. I personally thought that, if He did exist, He must not have known that I did.

"You sound surprised, Gia. I'm not that bad of a guy, you know." He laughed.

"I'm sorry, Sam. I didn't mean to say it like that. I just didn't know you went to church. That's all. It's cool."

"You want to come with us?"

"*Us?*" I took a hard gulp as if I swallowed a whole orange.

"Yeah, Dee's in the shower."

Dee was probably still high from the cocaine she sniffed at Ice. I guess cocaine addicts love Jesus too.

"I can't. I'm going to Westchester to see Micah."

"Oh, okay. I got to get up there with you one of these days."

"Yeah. He would love to see you, I'm sure," I said.

"Yeah, that's my boy. I'll try to come out there with you next time."

"Okay. I'll let him know you say hi. Well, I'm gonna get in the shower. I'll be back later tonight."

"Aight, G. Be safe out there." He picked his newspaper back up.

"I will." I headed to my room and got ready to go.

No matter what happened before I saw Micah, it magically disappeared when I saw him. He was the one person in my life that I could trust and that I loved.

"Gia." He gave me a bear hug when he saw me, lifting me off the ground.

"Hey, Mich. It's good to see you." I straightened out my clothes when my feet landed on the ground.

"You too, G. Nice hair! I don't think I've ever seen your hair down."

I touched my hair. "Yeah. I got a job where I have to wear it down."

"What kind of job tells you you have to wear your hair a certain way?" He turned up the corners of his mouth.

"I'm a guest list gir…or hostess. Whatever you want to

call it."

"At a club?" His face grew clouded.

"Yeah. I just started last night at Ice. It was cool. Good money," I said softly.

"I'm not really feeling my little sister at the clubs like that," he said, maintaining eye contact.

"It's cool. I work for a promoter, and he's cool. I'm staying with Sam and his girl, Dee."

"Aight. Sam's a good dude. I trust him. Just be careful at the clubs, G. I know you're grown and all, but men are not to be trusted. Always remember this. Men only want one thing — especially men at the clubs. No matter how nice they are to you, or what they say, or how much money they spend on you. They're hoping their niceness gets you in bed. They're hoping their words get you in bed, and they're hoping their money gets you in bed. They're all the same, and they're all liars, except for your big brother of course." He leaned back in his chair, smiling. "So, you speak to your mother lately?"

"I'm not going back there, Micah."

"I feel you, G. I know the situation, but she *is* your mother. Damn, I wish I could do more for you right now, G." He ran his palms up and down his thighs.

"Any new news from the lawyer, Mich?"

"I'm going to court in a couple of weeks. I'll know more then."

"Well, tell your lawyer he'll have to do better than that because your little sister graduates in four years, and she needs you at the graduation."

"Aight, Gia. I'll let him know."

"Speaking of school, you do the homework I gave you last time?" I smiled.

"Of course." He pulled the poem out of his pocket. He started to read slowly.

"Bananas ripe and green."

I interrupted him, "Title and author first, please."

"Oh, my fault. *The Tropics in New York* by Claude McKay[2]."

"Good."

He continued, "Bananas ripe and green, and gin...ginger."

"Gingerroot."

"Gingerroot. Cocoa in pods and alligat...alligator pears, and–" He took a deep breath.

"Take your time, Mich. You got it."

"Tang, tanger, tang-er-rines and mangoes and grapefruit, fit for the highest prize at par, par-ish, parish fairs."

"Great job, Mich."

"Can you finish it up, G?"

"Sure."

I read the poem from the beginning.

Bananas ripe and green, and gingerroot,
Cocoa in pods and alligator pears,
And tangerines and mangoes and grapefruit,
Fit for the highest prize at parish fair,
Set in the windows, bringing memories
Of fruit trees laden by low-singing rills,
And dewy dawns, and mystical blue skies
In benediction over nunlike hills.
My eyes grew dim, and I could no more gaze;
A wave longing through my body swept,
And hungry for the old, familiar ways,
I turned aside and bowed my head and wept.

I looked up at Micah. His eyes were closed, and he was nodding his head.

"I love the way you read, G. Your voice is so clear and soothing. It's like I'm there or something. Know what I mean?" He opened his eyes.

"Yeah." I smiled. "So, what do you think it's about?"

"Well, I think dude is missing home. Something he sees reminds him of all the things he's missing back where he's from."

"Exactly."

"Yo, G, how you find this stuff? How'd you get so smart?"

"Look who's talking. How'd *you* get so smart? You nailed that poem, Mich."

"I learned from the best." He smiled at me.

Our time was up before we knew it. After giving Micah another poem to read before our next visit, we hugged and said our goodbyes. On my way out, the guard gave me a folded piece of lined paper.

"It's from Jay," he said before I had the chance to ask. He avoided eye contact with me as if it would get him in trouble. I looked behind me. James was at the other side of the room and nodded his head. His baby's mother was heading toward me. I shoved the letter in my back pocket.

"Hey, Gina," she said.

"It's *Gia*," I corrected her.

"Sorry, Gia. You need a ride back to the Polo Grounds?" she asked.

I assumed that the letter had nothing to do with her and that I should probably keep my mouth shut.

"Yeah. Thanks." I followed her out.

She dropped me off in front of the Polo Grounds. I thought back to the question Micah asked about my mother. I looked up at my building, dismissed the thought of going upstairs, and walked to the train. I planned on buying a couple more dresses and one more pair of shoes with the money I made the previous night. Once I was finished shopping, I headed back uptown and took a quick nap before work.

11

MIXING BUSINESS WITH PLEASURE

That night I worked Lit. It was a small lounge in the West Village. The Sunday night crowd was much different from a Friday or Saturday crowd. Most of the people who partied on Sundays were business owners, athletes, artists, and musicians. A few nine-to-fivers looking to network came out on Sunday too.

My job was easy that night. The bouncer knew most of the industry people and escorted them inside. He passed the regular folk onto me, and that's when I did my thing.

The inside of Lit was much different than Ice. It was smaller. There was no dance floor but just as many VIP tables. Directly across from the VIP section was a long bar that extended the entire length of the club. The music was good, but people weren't dancing as much as they did at Ice. More people ordered bottles, which meant more money in my pocket by the end of the night.

Once the guest list closed, I went inside and checked up on the VIPs. I was often asked to sit down and have a drink. I'd agree to sit but not to drink. The questions were the same. Where you from, what do you do, are you single? But, there was something — someone — different at this particular table.

His name was Cliff. He sat at his table alone — no male entourage, no female groupies. It was just him and his bottle of champagne. When I asked if he was doing okay, he said, "Yeah, I'm good. I'm sorry, but I didn't catch your name."

"It's Gia," I said, shaking his hand.

"Wow, Gia, that's some handshake you got."

"So I've been told." I sat down.

"Okay, I like that. I'm Cliff, by the way. Nice to meet you."

Cliff looked to be in his late thirties. His glasses were oddly shaped, like squared-off circles, but they worked for the frame of his face. He wore a brown sweater with a plaid orange shirt underneath, dark blue jeans, and black Prada sneakers. They were different than the ones I saw the guys around the hood wearing. They looked as if he got them straight from Italy. I guess he caught me staring and read my mind.

"You like 'em?" He looked down at his sneakers. "I wasn't sure when I first tried them on. I couldn't understand anything the salesperson was saying. I'm not fluent in Italian, *yet* anyway."

I was turned off. He was pretentious and cocky.

"E' Un peccato!" It meant *what shame* in Italian. He put down his glass of champagne.

"You speak Italian?" he asked, surprised.

"A semester's worth. I always thought the language sounded so beautiful, so I took a class. As beautiful as it is, it isn't all that practical to learn. So next semester I'm considering Spanish or maybe even Arabic. Both are pretty practical."

"Um, yeah, I guess," he stuttered. "Where did you say you went to school?"

"I go to Brown in Rhode Island."

"Okay. Well, how long you in town for?"

"Just until the middle of January."

"So, I assume you're working the clubs for some extra money for school?"

"Yeah. Books are expensive."

"Aight, well you're obviously a smart girl. So, you understand that less hours for more money is smart. I own a management company. I work with the music industry's top artists. They're constantly looking for the next *it* girl for their videos. I think that your look and intelligence would come across beautifully on camera."

"I'm good on that one. I'm not gonna shake my ass for a couple of pennies and get treated like a piece of meat in the process. I make good enough money working for Ty."

"Well, have you been on the set of a music video before?" He slid his glasses up his nose.

"No, but I know what it's like."

"You sure you know?"

I wasn't but I saw enough music videos to know. I decided to stop watching them halfway through the semester when both men and women on campus assumed that, because I was black and from New York City, I'd act and look like the girls in the videos. I also didn't care for the music. Most songs were derogatory toward woman and spoke of a fake lifestyle that the artists themselves no longer lived. They were almost as hypocritical as people in church.

"If their art is an imitation of their lives, I don't want any part of it."

"All right, well how about this? Tomorrow, I'll be on the set of a Jahzelle video. Why don't you come through and just check it out? See how you feel about it. Here's my card. Call me tomorrow before noon, and I'll give you the details if you're interested." He handed me his business card.

I took it. Jahzelle was one of the hottest R&B artists out.

"Okay, fair enough." I hadn't decided yet if I was going to call or not, but I took the card anyway.

"I hope to hear from you tomorrow, Gia. But I need to get out of here. I have a long day tomorrow."

I looked at my watch. It was already three AM. We stood up simultaneously and shook hands. He headed toward the door, and I headed to the bar and sat next to Ty.

"How you like the Sunday crowd?" He motioned for the bartender.

"I like it. Much more laid back and professional."

"Can I get a bottled water?" he asked the bartender. "I thought you would. You're the sophisticated type." He took a sip of his Corona. "Another nice night, Gia."

He gave me $200 in cash. Added to the $100 I made in tips, I came away with $300 that night. I planned on giving some of the money to Sam. I'd been staying at his place for about a week and wanted to at least pay for the food I ate.

"Monday's your day off."

"I don't need a day off," I said, thinking of how much money I'd lose.

"I do! I'm tired. We're not all eighteen." He laughed. "I only work Mondays if there's a special event, and there's not tomorrow, so we're off. Anyway, you'll need to be good and rested up for Tuesday night."

"What's so special about Tuesday night?" I asked.

"It's Christmas Eve, which means that people don't have to go to work the next day, which means the club will be packed. We'll be working the Warehouse. You ever been there?"

I was tired of lying. "No. What's it like?"

"It's a lot different than here and Ice. We go for quantity over quality. The dress code is not as strict, and the lines get crazy. The cops usually show up and end up shutting the block down, but the party is crazy. The club is an old warehouse, so it can hold up to three thousand people. Because of that, there'll be other promoters and guest list girls there. So, I'll need you in the front until two AM as usual. I'll have a couple of girls inside getting names and e-mails for my mailing list. Once the guest list closes, I'll need you to come inside, and instead of doing the VIP thing, I need you to join the other two girls in getting names and e-mail addresses."

"But, who's going to take care of the VIP tables?"

"The waitresses will take care of that. I need you on the floors. It's an opportunity to grow my contacts. It's an opportunity for you too. I'm giving you and the other girls enough sheets to get five hundred names and e-mail addresses. If you get all five hundred names, that's an extra $100 in your pocket at the end of the night."

"I can do that. You have fliers I can hand out in the streets tomorrow since I have the day off and all?" I smiled.

"You know I have a street team that handles that, right?"

"I know. But, the more people who walk through that door on Tuesday night, the more money in my pocket."

"True, true. Aight. I don't have any on me. They're in my car." He looked at his watch. "Stay here. I'll be right back."

I took a sip of my water as he walked to the back of the club. He returned with our coats.

"The party's dying down." He handed me my coat. "You hungry?"

"Yeah. But, I'm taking the train, so I should be heading back uptown."

I took a cab back the first night but decided that I didn't want to get in the habit of paying $25 a night for transportation when I could ride the subway for $2.

"I'll drive you home." He took the last sip of his Corona.

"But, you live all the way in Brooklyn, and we're in the Village. My place is out of your way. I can take the train."

"Gia, we have the day off tomorrow. I can sleep in all day if I want to. I'll take you home. Anyway, I'm craving breakfast and don't want to eat alone."

"Okay." I was hungry and hated waiting for the train so late at night anyway.

"Cool. My car is on 6th. We'll go the Chelsea Diner," he said, tipping the bartender.

I shivered when the cold air stung my bare legs. I crossed my arms and rubbed them vigorously, hoping to warm myself. My futile attempt didn't go unnoticed. He took off his coat and slung it around my shoulders.

"Thanks, Ty, but you'll freeze. I'm good." I took his coat off my shoulders.

"Nah, keep it. We need to protect those pretty little legs from the cold. They're making me good money." He looked down at my legs.

My cheeks suddenly felt warm. "Yeah, whatever," I said as he put his coat back over my shoulders. I heard his phone vibrate. I glanced over his shoulder and looked at it as he did. It was Terrance. He hit ignore and kept walking. I assumed he was calling to get my number. I hadn't thought much about it since I'd met him the other night. I figured Ty either didn't want to be rude by talking on his phone while he was with me or that he just didn't feel like talking to Terrance right then and there.

"I'm right here." He pointed to a black Infiniti parked on the corner. He pressed the button on his key chain, disabling the alarm. I checked my hair and makeup in the reflection of the shiny, black paint. Goose bumps ran down my legs when they hit the cold leather seats. The car was spotless inside and out and smelled of cologne. The car commanded attention without being ostentatious. It was well-made, classy, and smooth — just like Ty.

John Legend's *Save Room* played from the speakers.

"Good taste." I tapped the balls of my feet on the floor mats.

"You like R&B?" He started the car.

"Yeah. I like all different types of music as long as the lyrics are on point."

"Who are some of your favorite artists?" We were catching all the green lights on 6th Avenue.

"For rap, Kanye, Common, Talib, Jada."

"Oh, you on a first-name basis, huh?" He turned on the windshield wipers. "How about R&B?"

"I love R&B. Alicia Keys, India.Arie, Jill Scott, Ne-yo, Aretha Franklin, Luther Vandross, Al Green."

"What you know about Al Green, girl? That's before your time."

"Yeah, well, good music is timeless."

"True, true," he said as he turned onto 23rd Street.

"Nice parking," I commented on his parallel parking.

"Yeah, I'm pretty nice with it. You know you gotta be in this city. If you're lucky, I'll let you drive home." He smiled.

"Nah, I'm good on that one. I don't have a license and I've never been behind the wheel of a car."

"So? What better way to learn than in the best city in the world? Besides, I trust you Gia." He turned off the ignition and looked into my eyes.

"I'm glad you do because I don't trust myself," I said, looking deeper into his eyes and pressing my lips together.

"Oh, word?"

"Word." I stepped out of the car.

The diner was packed. It was a well-known New York City after-hours spot. Because it was in Chelsea close to all of the clubs, it usually got crowded around four or five AM. Club goers hungry from a night of dancing went there to fuel up. To others, it was an infirmary — the place to start nursing an impending hangover. It was affectionately nicknamed Get Lucky's because most men saw it as their last chance to bag any last-minute phone numbers or jump-offs for the night.

"Two please," I said to the host.

He sat us at a booth facing 23rd Street. I looked out the window and watched the moon and sun change shifts.

"Most people are just getting up to go to work, and we're just finishing." Ty followed my gaze out the window.

"Yeah. How did you get into the club thing anyway?" I took the wrapper off of my straw.

"After I graduated high school, I went to City College. I never really wanted to go to college, but all my teachers gave me the same old speech. Tyrone, you're smart. Go to college. Make something of yourself. In my heart, I knew I didn't need college to be successful. Don't get me wrong. I respect any brother or sister who decides to go to college. It's just not for everyone. And there are plenty of people who made something of themselves who didn't go to college. You know what I'm saying, G?"

"Yeah, I hear you," I agreed. "But as time goes on, those people are fewer and farther between. These days, you can't even be a secretary without a degree."

"You ready to order?" the waiter interrupted.

We didn't have a chance to look at the menu. We were talking from the moment we sat down. I knew what I wanted anyway.

"BLT and fries for me." I handed the menu to the waiter. "Oh, and a glass of orange juice."

"You eat pork, Gia?" Ty asked, surprised.

"Yeah, and?" I asked, irritated. "Let me guess. You don't?" I rolled my eyes.

"Nah, I don't. Let me get oatmeal with granola and a fruit salad." He looked up at the waiter.

"Anything to drink, sir?"

"Coffee. Black, please." Ty handed over his menu.

"Certainly." The waiter walked away with our menus and orders.

"Oatmeal? You really are a part of the back-to-Africa crew, aren't you, Ty?"

"The back-to-Africa crew? What the hell is that?" he asked,

sipping his water.

"You know. Back to Africa, neo-soul, dirty backpacks, red, green, and black wristband-wearing type of black folks. The dreads, vegetarian food, smoke a spliff every now and then to ease your mind and tap into your *creative side*."

"Who said I smoke, Gia?" He looked across the table into my eyes.

"Come on now, Ty. We've spent the last two nights together. I know these things. I'm good at reading people. And get off my back about my BLT. Alcohol is more of a poison than pork will ever be. Black people smoke cigarettes and any other type of mess you give them, drink all types of alcohol, have all types of unprotected sex with God knows who, but they gonna talk about 'I don't eat swine?' Please!"

"You think you got a brother all figured out, huh? So, since you know so much, I guess I don't need to tell you the rest of my story."

"I'll finish it for you," I said.

This was going to be easy. I knew everything I needed to know about Ty within the first ten minutes of meeting him.

"You already told me you tried the college thing, and it wasn't for you."

"Uh huh." He placed his elbows on the table and leaned in.

"Well, you always knew you wanted to be an entrepreneur. When you were little, you'd buy candy from the corner store for fifty cents and sell it to your classmates for a dollar. As a teenager, you could've started hustling, but that wasn't a challenge enough, and too many people were doing it. You wanted to stand apart from the crowd. You knew you were more talented than slinging rocks in a hood that you would inevitably get stuck in if you decided to go that route. You were always mature for your age, so you started to go to the clubs young. It started as fun and a thrill, but then your thought process changed and you started to see it as a business opportunity. The thought of starting your own club appealed to you, but you didn't want to be tied down to one spot seven days a week. So you started promoting. You made a name for yourself and decided you'd make more money if you owned your own promotion company — thus the birth of Sapphire Entertainment."

The waiter came out with our food. "BLT for the lady, oatmeal for the gentleman." He placed our plates in front of us.

"Thanks," I said as he left the table.

Ty wiped the sweat off his forehead with his napkin. He looked down and avoided eye contact.

"I'm speechless. You damn sure weren't playing."

His phone started vibrating again. He glanced at it and hit ignore.

"It's cool if you need to answer that." I picked up my BLT, anxious to take a bite.

"Nah, it's not important. I'll call 'em back later." He ate a spoonful of oatmeal and looked up at me. "So, let me guess. You're a psychology major?"

"No. I'm an artist, but haven't decided on a major yet. I did take a psychology class first semester, but it didn't teach me much that I didn't already know."

"You got a gift, Gia. You don't strike me as the type who can't decide on a major. You seem like a woman who knows what she wants and takes it."

"You're right about that," I said. "I love art and literature. When I was in high school, I'd lock myself in my bedroom for hours and paint. My art teacher would hook me up with old tubes of paint. I'd use brown paper lunch bags, newspaper, even toilet paper as canvas. I spent a lot of my free time either painting or reading, but I know I can't make much of a living out of either. So, during my first semester, I took a bunch of subjects that I found art in but that were practical."

"I'm confused," he said.

"There's art in everything. You just need to pay attention to find it. I took Italian because the sound of the language was an auditory art in itself. I took American literature because good prose paints a picture that is unique for the reader. I took anatomy because the human body is the most fascinating work of art imaginable. I took psychology because it's an extension of the human body, and I took sociology because the way people meet and interact with each other is like great art — sometimes it's beautiful, disturbing, or difficult to explain."

"In all my years on this earth, I can honestly say I don't ever think I've heard anything like that." He stared at his oatmeal as if it were speaking to him.

It was the first time I had ever shared so much with a stranger in such a short amount of time. I was beginning to regret it. We ate quietly for the rest of the meal. I asked how his oatmeal was and he said it was good and looked away. He seemed to avoid eye contact for the remainder of the meal, so I followed suit.

I ate fast. The quicker I finished my meal, the quicker I could go home and sleep. Thinking of sleep reminded me of how tired I was. I decided not to take offense to Ty's attitude. He was probably just as tired as I was.

"You ready to get out of here, Gia?" He wiped his mouth.

"Yeah." I stood up. "Hey, Ty, I'm sorry if I said anything that made you upset."

I wanted to smooth things over just in case. Ty's feelings weren't all that important to me, but my job was.

"Nah, Gia. Everything's cool. I'm just really tired. You're cool."

"Okay. Oh, and by the way, I hope you don't mind. I took some flyers for the Christmas Eve party from the backseat of your car. I'm going to hand some out now."

He looked surprised. "I think you work even harder than I do." He smiled.

"Maybe. You can go out to the car. I'll be right there. I'm

going to hand these out." I fanned through the flyers with my thumb.

"Okay. Cool."

He headed to the car, and I took the next five minutes to give party fliers out to every single table. I was only going to be in town for three more weeks and needed every penny I could get. I was not too proud to interrupt people's breakfasts to invite them to the club. I even got a couple of telephone numbers in return. I walked to Ty's car, and he drove me uptown.

"You going to be okay to drive all the way back out to Brooklyn, Ty?"

"Are you inviting me in, Gia?" He smiled.

I got nervous.

"I would, but this isn't my place. I'm staying with a friend until I get back to school."

"It's cool. I was only playing. But, I'm good to drive to Brooklyn. This is what I do, Gia. Get in safe." He unlocked the doors.

"Okay."

He leaned in close the way he did in Macy's at the Mac counter, but this time, instead of my neck, he went for my cheek and kissed it respectfully.

"Get some rest tomorrow. You've made me a lot of money over the last two nights, and I need you to be on for Tuesday."

"I will be. Good night."

I got to the front door of Sam's building and looked back. Ty was watching me. I waved goodbye, and he drove off.

Despite my exhaustion, I decide to check my e-mails. I had several from Stephen. The first was dated a couple of days after I left school.

Gia,

I tried calling your apartment. I hope you don't mind. I got the number from a friend of mine who works in the registrar's office. My

cell number is 508-555-7119.
   Stephen.

The second was sent the day after I left Stephen at the restaurant.

Gia,
   *I'm really sorry if I did anything to make you upset the other night.
I didn't mean to hurt you or make you upset. I was really excited to
see you. I miss you.*
   Stephen.

I thought back to the first time I'd heard Stephen say that. He'd organized a charity softball game to raise money for a local family shelter. Several of the families were there participating in the event. It was a battle of the sexes, and Stephen and I were in the dugout. He shouted, encouraging the player up at bat. The boy hit a home run. Stephen and the rest of the team went wild. Out of breath, he sat down beside me.

"Looks like your team is really serious about the win," I said.

"Yeah. Really doesn't matter who wins or who loses. I'm just glad so many people showed up and we raised some money. And the kids look like they're really having fun. Kids like these really deserve it." He shifted in his seat and hesitated before he spoke again. "I mean a lot of these kids are poor – and – well I just want them to have all the good things they deserve."

I focused my attention to the game. There was an awkward silence.

After a few minutes Stephen said, "I'm really sorry if I said something that made you upset. The last thing I would ever want to do is upset you Gia."

"You didn't Stephen. Don't sweat it."

My fingers hovered over the keyboard. Instead of responding to the emails, I deleted them.

12

ANOTHER JOB OPPORTUNITY

Taking Ty's advice, I decided to sleep in. When I woke up at eleven AM, Sam was at work and Dee was out. I rubbed my eyes and looked at my room. It was a mess. There were clothes all over the place. I put my dresses in a pile to be dry-cleaned and the rest of my dirty clothes in a pile to go to the laundry mat. As I threw a pair of jeans in the laundry pile, a piece of paper flew out. I unfolded and read it.

The keys to the Benz could be yours if you'd only let me put them in your hands. I'm out of here in a couple of days. I'll be checking for you around the hood. Call me. 646-555-6839. James aka Jay.

I completely forgot about the note the guard at the jail slipped me. James might be checking for me, but I sure as hell would not be checking for him. I crumpled up the note and threw it in the wastebasket next to my dresser.

I headed to the kitchen and poured a glass of orange juice. I sat at the table and thought about what it was that I wanted to do on my day off.

I planned on seeing Micah on Christmas Day. I considered going to my mother's apartment to get all of my belongings. I wanted to remove anything that could later be used as an excuse for going back. I had a couple of pictures of my grandmother, my high school diploma, and achievement awards that I wanted to get. Anything else that was of any value I already counted as a loss. My mother probably had stolen and sold it.

After finishing my orange juice, I went back to my room and organized the business cards I'd collected at the diner. I regretted throwing the ones I got at Ice away. I planned on using them all to invite people out to the party on Tuesday night. I stopped at one of the cards and picked up my cell.

"Clifford Hicks. Eternity Artist Management." I read the card out loud to myself. "Well, I have nothing better to do today. Why not?" I looked at my alarm clock. Eleven thirty AM. It was before noon, exactly when he asked me to call.

"Hello, this is Cliff," he answered.

"Hi, Cliff. It's Gia. I met you at Lit the other night."

"No need to remind me, Gia. It'd be impossible to forget a beautiful face like yours. I was hoping you'd call. You planning on coming by the shoot today?"

"Yeah. I have the night off, so my day is pretty free." I held up the phone with my shoulder while shuffling through the other business cards.

"Okay, cool. Well, we're shooting on the Upper East Side. We'll be on 64th between Park and Lexington. It's a residential street with a bunch of brownstones. You can't miss the camera crew. They'll probably have the street blocked off. Just call me when you get there, and I'll escort you through."

"Okay. What time should I be there?" I asked.

"They start shooting at two PM."

"Okay. I'll be there. 64th between Park and Lex at two."

"You got it. I'll see you there."

"All right, Cliff."

I hung up, put the business cards away, and headed to the shower. I stopped short when I saw Dee in the hall. She wasn't alone. There was a man with her.

It wasn't Sam.

They were both carrying two large duffel bags. I had gotten in so late that I wasn't sure if she had spent the night in the apartment or not. I glared at her.

She rolled her eyes and brushed passed me to the bedroom.

I looked the man up and down. His eyes were blank, and there was dirt underneath his fingernails. Now, I definitely didn't trust Dee. She was a fiend and a cheater. Did she really have the nerve to bring some other man up in Sam's apartment? I grunted at him and walked into the bathroom. Before I started the shower, I heard them attempting to whisper to each other.

"Yo, Dee, you stay leaving out important details. Who the hell is she?" he asked in a heavy Spanish accent.

"Don't worry about her. She's only here for a little while. She's harmless. And, she knows to keep her mouth shut," Dee said.

I started the shower. I wanted to get out of there. I didn't want Dee trying to follow me to the shoot. I didn't know what she was up to, but I knew it couldn't be anything good. As the days went on, I became more and more uncomfortable around her. We barely spoke. At the end of the day, she knew I wouldn't say anything out of fear of getting kicked out of the apartment. But, living with her was causing me to question my safety.

I scrubbed my body, attempting to rub away my negative feelings about Dee. I was determined to stay focused for the next couple of weeks. The goal was to make a little bit of money to get me back to school, and I'd be damned if someone as insignificant as Dee was going to stop me.

I wasn't sure what I should wear to a video shoot. Although it was unseasonably warm for December in New York, it was still a good twenty-five degrees too cold for open-toed shoes. It was okay for the clubs, but wearing open-toed shoes in mid-December would get me nothing but cold stares and cold toes. Sneakers were not an option. Luckily, before I went to work the previous day, I'd picked up a pair of brown boots that came up just below my knees. They had two-inch heels that were high enough to be sexy but low enough to be comfortable.

I decided on a tight, brown sweater dress, brown tights, and my green down jacket with the fur-trimmed hood. The green went well with the brown and kept the outfit casual. The black coat I wore to the clubs would have dressed the outfit up more than I wanted to.

I wore my hair down and decided against a ton of makeup. Instead, I opted for a pink lip gloss and mascara. That was enough. I grabbed my purse and headed out.

✱✱✱

Even without the decorations inside storefronts or music coming from the street musicians, there was a uniquely New York spirit of Christmas in the air. I walked toward the video set, letting my imagination wander behind the walls of the multi-million dollar brownstones that lined the street. I imagined a towering, fresh-cut Christmas tree in the living room, saturating the air with the smell of fresh pine. I inhaled deeply and closed my eyes. The stair banister would be dressed in red-and-green tinsel and white Christmas lights. Some presents under the tree were big and wrapped in paper that looked like winter, adorned with baby-blue bows and glittering snowflakes. Others were small, wrapped in the colors of Christmas.

A horn blared. I stopped short and opened my eyes. The image faded. The reality of the Christmases I'd experienced after my grandmother's death was much different than my imagination. The only decoration in our apartment was a wreath I'd made out of a paper plate and macaroni noodles that I'd given to my grandmother as a child but inherited back after she died. She'd faithfully hung it in the living room every Christmas. The Christmas after she died, I hung it my bedroom. After waking up to no presents on that Christmas morning, I put the wreath in my closet and never celebrated another Christmas.

I saw the lights and cameras as soon as I reached 64th and Park. My heart raced, and my pace followed as I approached a crowd of people. I unexpectedly grew excited and nervous. I wasn't really sure why. Part of me couldn't believe that I'd made the decision to come. It was understatement to say I wasn't excited about coming home a couple weeks ago. I was expecting to work for a couple of weeks to make enough money to pay for my books. I'd already made enough for that, and now I was being offered an opportunity to make even more.

I always believed that anything that was too good to be true either wasn't or that it'd only be a matter of time before it went sour. In the back of my mind, I was always waiting for the rug to be pulled from underneath my feet. The trick was staying on my toes. That way, I wouldn't fall as hard.

As Cliff warned me, there were two NYPD officers standing on opposite sides of a wooden barricade at the entrance to the street. I had my cellphone and could have easily called Cliff. Instead, I walked through the crowd with my head held high. I put an extra switch in my step, tossed my hair over my shoulder, and looked both officers in the eyes. One got on a walkie-talkie, nodded his head yes, and moved the barricade aside. I walked right through. I heard people in the crowd asking why I was so special. I smiled at the control I had. As I got closer to the set, I slowed my pace and looked for Cliff. Someone approached me immediately.

"You're late. Where have you been?" The woman put her hand on my shoulder and forced me to walk faster. "Head over to hair and makeup in that trailer closer to Lexington."

"Oh, you've got the wrong person. I'm just here to watch. I'm not one of the models."

She looked me up and down. "Oh. Well, you damn sure look like one."

The thought that Cliff invited me here for his own personal gain crossed my mind once again. Being mistaken for one of the models led me to think maybe Cliff was serious about me being in the video.

Suddenly, I felt a hand on my shoulder. It was Cliff.

"Hey, Gia," he said and immediately introduced me to the woman who was one of the casting directors for the shoot. "This is Gia, the girl I was telling you about."

"Ah! Nice to meet you, Gia. Sorry about that. Our lead girl is late, and at a quick glance, I thought you might be her."

"It's okay." I tucked my hair behind my ear.

"Excuse me, I need to find out where she is. Don't go too far though. I want to talk to you before we wrap today." She looked back and talked over her shoulder as she bounced away.

"Okay," I said.

Cliff looked down at his phone. "Gia, how'd you get through? You didn't call me."

"I didn't need to. I just walked through like I belonged here, and they let me in." I smiled.

"All right, Gia." He laughed. "I guess they were thinking exactly the same thing the casting director was."

"Yeah, I guess." I acted unfazed.

"So, here's the deal. This is Jahzelle's second single off

his sophomore album. His first album went double platinum, and so did the first single off this album. So, we're hoping to see the same success here. The video is everything — kids watch and request it on 106 & Park, they watch it on YouTube, they download it from iTunes, and the rest is history. That's why today's so important. And, that's why you're so important. Young men want to be Jahzelle because they see him with beautiful women in the video. Young ladies want to be you because they see you with Jahzelle in the video, and they want to be with Jahzelle."

I had to interject. "That's ridiculous." I crossed my arms in front of my chest. "The girls in these videos are paid actors. People aren't that mindless. They don't associate what they see in a video with what actually happens in real life, do they?"

"Shhh." He put his fingers to his lips and looked around. "Don't say that too loud," he joked. "Of course it's ridiculous. But, it's proven. A good video equals good record sales. Who are we to mess with that formula? Especially when that formula gets us both paid."

"I guess." I still thought it was crazy. The thought of getting paid, on the other hand, wasn't all that crazy. But, there was only so much I would do for money. To me, there was a fine line between being in a video and being a ho and a prostitute. Both sold sex.

"So, can I tell you how I think you fit into all of this?" He walked me down the street.

"That's why you invited me here, right?" I asked.

"Smart girl. I don't see you in rap videos. I see you in R&B, pop, and even rock videos. You're too pretty and too well put together to be an extra. You have a silent strength that commands attention and a presence that's reserved for a leading role." He looked up at the sky as if it were the big screen. I looked up and saw nothing.

"Yeah, and I've seen a lot of girls in the leading roles who do the same old things. At the end of the day, they all still end up shaking their asses."

"Not necessarily. The storyboard's been written for this video. You want to see it?" He pushed his glasses up the bridge of his nose.

"Okay," I said, genuinely interested in seeing it.

He led me past the lights, cameras, and crew to one of the trailers in the back. This particular trailer was reserved for the crew. It was crowded with extra equipment. There was a man working on a computer in the corner.

"Hey, man. This is Gia. She's working on the shoot today. Can I give her a look at the storyboard?"

"Hey, Gia. Good to meet you. No problem."

He pressed a couple of buttons on his Mac and pulled up a file. He explained the setup of the video.

"See, Gia. This song is about a man who genuinely loved a woman and lost her because of his infidelity."

"Wow, that's unique," I said sarcastically.

He looked at me. "I like this one, Cliff. I agree, but if it ain't broke, don't fix it, right? And it ain't broke yet. Anyway, we're only shooting a few scenes this afternoon. The first half of the day, we're with Jahzelle and his leading lady, the one who eventually gets away, at their home. There'll be the typical shots on the stoop heading out to start the day, in the kitchen cooking for each other in their pajamas, and of course, the lovemaking scene."

"I was waiting for that one," I said, wanting to say *I told you so* to Cliff. I refrained out of fear of sounding juvenile.

"Can you please tell this young lady what's involved in that particular scene? She thinks that, by being in these videos, she'll be selling her soul to the devil."

"I didn't say all that, Cliff. I don't even believe in the devil. But if one did exist, he would damn sure be a man."

They both laughed. I didn't.

"Well in this particular video, the scene is tasteful. The woman will be in a black lace bra and boy shorts. When it looks as if it's about to get raunchy, Jahzelle grabs a pillow and starts a pillow fight. The whole relationship between Jahzelle and the lead is a romantic one, but the director really wants to convey their friendship. The sex that sells this particular video is left up to the extras who play the women Jahzelle ends up ruining his relationship over."

It didn't sound bad, but I'd believe it when I saw it. Besides, this one role was probably the exception to the rule. And I wasn't even cast as the lead.

The door swung open. It was the casting director.

"Hey, guys," she said, breathing heavily. "Hey, what's your name again?" she snapped at me.

"It's Gia," I snapped back.

"Gia, you ever work a video before?"

"No."

"Well, how do you feel about being in your first video... today. Now!" She was obviously on edge and wanted an immediate answer.

"Um," I hesitated. "There are no extras on set who could–"

"Not today there aren't. It was just our lead girl and Jahzelle who were scheduled to shoot today. And she's nowhere to be found."

"I, umm..." I was nervous and speechless. I never acted a day in my life. I only learned how to walk in heels a couple of days ago, and I had never been romantically intimate with a man in any kind of way in any kind of setting. My lack of experience was sure to come across on camera. I always heard the camera never lies. But, how hard could it really be? And if they asked me to do anything I was uncomfortable with, I could bail. They were the ones who needed me. I didn't need them.

I looked at Cliff again. I must have had a terrified look on my face. He gave me a warm smile and nodded his head yes in encouragement.

"Well, how much will I get paid if I do?"

"It's a flat rate of $1,000 for the rest of today. If they need you on other days, they'll pay you for that time too," Cliff answered.

"Actually, Cliff, the price was negotiated at $800 for the day," the casting director said.

"Yeah, that was the other girl's rate. Gia's rate is $1,000."

She looked unhappy at Cliff's request, but she was obviously in a crunch.

"Okay, Gia. Will you do it for $1,000?" she asked.

I assumed that, by demanding a higher price, Cliff was probably intending on getting a cut. I also assumed that by her *asking* if I would do it for $1,000, the rate was negotiable.

"$1,500, and I'll head over to hair and makeup right now."

I decided that, if I was going to step foot in this game, I'd go all in. Cliff frowned and shook his head. The production assistant looked as if this was the highlight of his day. The casting director's phone rang. Lines formed on her forehead.

"Hold on." She answered her phone. "Yeah?" She paused. "I have no idea where she is. I called her a million times. She's not picking up her phone." She closed her eyes and took a deep breath. "I have another model here who's going to do it. She's in hair and makeup right now." Another pause. "Yeah. Yeah. Uh huh. Yeah, bye," she said quickly and hung up.

"The rate is $1,500 for today."

"Point me toward hair and makeup," I said.

She led me to another trailer. There was makeup everywhere. I grew nauseated at the thought of all that makeup on my face. I knew it would only be temporary though, so I kept my mouth shut.

"Gia, this is Alicia. She'll be doing your makeup. Chris will be in to do your hair, and Paulina will be taking care of wardrobe. They'll be here in about twenty minutes. What size are you? About a six?"

"Yeah."

"Okay." She was off again.

"Should I sit in the chair?" I pointed to the chair in front of me.

"Yeah, have a seat." Alicia smiled. I sat down and faced a large mirror surrounded by bright lights that caused me to squint.

"Is this your first video, Gia?" Alicia asked.

"Yeah," I laughed nervously. "Can you tell?"

"Not really. You look the part. You have the nicest skin I've seen in a long time."

"Thanks."

"Okay, so I'll let you know the instruction I got from the producer. For the first scene, your makeup is going to be really light. We'll do some foundation, a little mascara and eyeliner, and we'll do a really natural gloss." She talked at my reflection.

"Okay, that's cool," I said as she took out the makeup.

As promised, Chris and Paulina were there soon after Alicia started my makeup. I thought Chris was short for Christina, but it was short for Christopher. He was dark-skinned, bald, and chubby and had more energy than a can of Red Bull.

"I guess you would be Gina," he stated.

"Actually, I'm Gia. You're Chris?" I asked.

"That's me, honey. It's nice to meet you." He squashed the small talk and got right to business. "Let me see this hair."

He shooed Alicia away. She laughed and positioned herself directly in front of my face to finish my makeup.

"Oh, girl. My job's going to be easy today. You have a fresh wash and set, I see. Mmm-hmm. Well, for this scene, we're going to keep you very natural. You'll have your hair in a loose pony. We'll give you a part on the side and have a long bang swoop down loose to your left eye and tucked behind your ear. Alicia how long before you finish her makeup?" he asked, massaging my scalp.

"I'll be done in about twenty minutes," Alicia answered.

"All right. I'll be right back, ya'll. I gots to get my tool-box." He floated out of the trailer. I couldn't help but smile.

"Girl, Chris is a hot mess. When he does your hair, he will talk your ear off for sure," Alicia warned me.

"It's cool. I don't mind. Just as long as he doesn't jack up my hair, we're good."

She laughed. I didn't.

"I heard that!" Chris was already back with a large black suitcase in his hand. He placed the suitcase on top of the sofa and rummaged through it.

"The other model done missed out!" He pulled out a blow dyer. "You know what they say. You sleep, and you don't eat!" Next he pulled out a curling iron.

"You both worked with her before?" I asked.

"Yeah, girl," Chris answered. "She's in all the big videos. See, the veterans think these jobs are promised to them. They show up late, act like they don't give a damn on set, and all the while, a million other pretty girls are waiting to take their place."

"I don't see what the big deal is. Get here on time, look pretty for a couple of scenes, and you get paid. Easy money, right?"

"Be prepared, girl. These shoots can be really long some-times," Alicia said. "It can get tiring having people shout or-ders at you to do the same thing over and over." She applied a light coat of blush as she talked.

"I guess." I wasn't convinced that the job was all that difficult.

"This your first video, Gia?" Chris asked.

"Yeah." That question always made me nervous. I didn't know if it was painfully obvious that I was a rookie or if I appeared to be so calm that they thought I'd done it before.

"Did you meet Jahzelle yet?" Chris asked.

"No."

"Girl, he is so fine all right!"

I laughed harder than I expected to.

"You're composed for a rookie. Girl, you know how many girls would kill to meet Jahzelle?" Chris asked.

"Yeah, I know. But I don't understand the big fascination with celebrities. The only difference between Jahzelle and me is that his talents make him more money than mine do, and they cause him to be in the public eye, and mine don't."

Alicia smiled, "I like the way you think."

Chris laughed. "All right, girl. I'll give you that. But let's see if you're as cool when he flashes that million dollar smile at you. Mmmmm-hmmmm." We all laughed.

"All right, Chris," said Alicia, stepping away from the chair. "I'm done." I looked good. There was more than a little bit of makeup on my face, a lot more than the makeup artist put on me at the Mac counter at Macy's.

"Umm, I thought you said the makeup was going to be light, Alicia."

"Yeah. That is light. When those lights hit you, you'll look washed out if you don't have enough makeup on. The other scenes call for a lot more. Trust me. This is light."

"All right," I said as Chris walked over to start on my hair.

"So, Gia. How you book this job?"

"Well, I kind of just fell into it to be honest with you. I met Jahzelle's manager the other night at my job and–"

"Where you work at, girl?" Chris asked.

"Well, while I'm off from school, I'm working in the clubs."

He stopped combing my hair and looked into my eyes. "Girl, is you a stripper?"

"Hell no!" I said, offended.

"Okay, I just got to ask. A lot of girls who've sat in this very chair were former strippers. It's not far-fetched." He batted his eyelashes and whipped the comb around in the air.

"Well, I'm not. I'm a college student. But, while I'm here in New York, I'm working as a hostess in a couple clubs. Actually, I'm hosting a party tomorrow night. You two should come." I reached in my bag for the fliers. I gave one to both Chris and Alicia.

"Ain't you cute," Chris joked, not even looking at the flyer and putting it down on the counter. "So, go on." He parted my hair.

"So, anyway. I was hosting a party the other night at Lit in the Village. I met Jahzelle's manager there, and he invited me on set today. I had nothing better to do so I came. I was really just here to see what it was like, and when the other girl didn't show, I was offered the job. And here I am."

"See that? Someone is always waiting to take your place." Chris waved the brush in the air as Paulina walked in.

"Hey, I'm Paulina. You must be Gia."

"Nice to meet you." I shook her hand.

"Sorry, Chris. But I need her to stand up for a minute."

"No problem," Chris said.

I stood up and did a 360. "I'm a six," I said, anticipating her question.

"Okay. Once Chris finishes up your hair, just walk over to the rack. I'll be waiting for you."

She walked to the other end of the trailer where clothes hung from racks on caster wheels. I sat back in the chair and waited as Chris finished my hair.

The way I transformed over the last hour was unbelievable. The light makeup that Alicia promised wasn't so light after all, and the hair was simple but sexy.

I thanked Chris and Alicia and headed over to Paulina at the racks. There were a lot of clothes. There were casual looks — jeans and graphic Ts. There were dressy looks — club attire and cocktail dresses. And then, there were the shoes. There must have been about twenty pairs. There were sneakers, sandals, stilettos, and even slippers.

"All right, Gia. Now for the first scene you're shooting today, you'll be wearing pajamas."

I got nervous. I knew at some point there would be a bedroom scene, but I didn't think it would be the first scene I was shooting. I tried to conceal my nerves.

"Okay, so what will I be wearing?" I asked. Paulina pulled something from the rack. It was a man's button-down shirt.

"Here. Try this on." I looked around for a dressing room. There wasn't one. I looked over at Chris.

"Oh please, miss honey child. You ain't got nothin I wanna see."

"Neither do you, Chris," I snapped back.

"Meow!" He pretended his hand was a cat's paw about to scratch. I shook my head and smiled.

I undressed and put on the shirt. Paulina helped me button it, leaving the top two buttons undone. It fit loose but showed off my curves.

"Perfect." Paulina looked me up and down. "I think we'll go barefoot for this scene."

"Okay." I pulled off my shoes and socks. The pedicure I got a couple of days ago was still perfectly intact.

"This'll work," Paulina said. There was a knock on the door.

"Come in," Chris yelled.

I stood behind the door, unable to see who it was. By the excitement in Chris's voice, I assumed it was Jahzelle.

"Everyone decent?" His voice was masculine but sultry. Although I had only heard it on the radio and on television, it was unmistakably his.

"Yeah. Come in, Jah," Paulina said. He saw Paulina before he saw me.

"Hey, Paulina." He walked toward her.

"Hey, Jah."

They hugged. He turned toward me, and his face lit up.

"Wow." He looked me over and smiled. "You're not–"

I interrupted him, "No, I'm Gia. Nice to meet you."

We shook hands. His smile was perfection. I'd never seen anything like it. His lips were full and moist. His teeth were so white that they sparkled the way snow does when the sun hits it.

Although he was shorter than I expected, he commanded attention. He was five-foot-eleven with a medium build. His skin was the color of hot chocolate. His hair was fine and jet black. It was neatly braided in corn rows. Looking at him and hearing his voice caused an unfamiliar feeling to consume my body. I felt my cheeks getting warm. I knew I was blushing, but no one else did. My brown skin and the pound of makeup on my face did a good job of concealing that. My heart beat faster than usual. I rubbed my hands against my thighs to rid them of the sweat that formed on my palms. I was determined to make this a business-only relationship. I didn't like that meeting Jah for the first time had caused my body to react the way it did.

"Sorry, Jah. I don't usually come to work in my pajamas. But, I thought you might be cool with it. You seem like a pretty laid-back guy on TV so...." I prayed that my joke would break the ice. It did. He laughed.

"It's all good, Gia. You look good in 'em, and that's all that matters."

There was that smile again. I was tempted to say something rude just to make him stop smiling. I didn't know how much longer I'd be able to resist it.

"What other videos you been in, Gia?" he asked.

"This is my first." I recognized the quavering in my voice.

"Oh, word?" He sounded worried.

"Yeah." I didn't know what I could say to convince him that I'd do a good job. I couldn't even convince myself.

"All right. Well, good luck. I'll see you on set in a couple minutes."

"All right." I took a deep breath.

"Told you he was fine, girl. Mmm-hmmm." Chris packed up his suitcase. I ignored him.

"Okay, so slip on these flip-flops and that robe, and let's head over to the set," Paulina instructed.

Forty-five degrees felt like five degrees in flip-flops and bare legs. Luckily, the cold was only temporary. I shuffled to the house as fast as I could.

The first scene took place in the kitchen. It wasn't a studio but an actual full-sized kitchen inside of a brownstone that I assumed was rented for the shoot. It was the largest and nicest kitchen I'd ever seen in a New York City apartment — or ever for that matter. The countertops were granite and the stovetop sat on an island in the middle of the kitchen. A hood hung above the stove and was decorated with pots and pans. All the appliances were stainless steel.

The director walked in with other members of the crew and introduced himself.

"You must be Gia," he said. "Nice to meet you."

"Hi, nice to meet you," I said, distracted. The crew that accompanied him pulled items out of the fridge and placed them on tiny duct-taped Xs that were taped to the countertop near the stove. He barked directions at me.

"All right, Gia. Here's the deal. In this scene, Jah is rem-iniscing about the beautiful times he had with the perfect woman, that's you, by the way, who eventually becomes the one who got away. So, when I yell *action*, act like you're cook-ing eggs and have no idea that Jah is standing in the doorway behind your back looking at you and, well, singing at you. We'll shoot you cooking the eggs for one verse of the song. Then, we'll shoot you and Jah cooking together. He'll be standing behind you, close to you, looking over your shoul-der. His hands will be near your waist, and he'll hold his hand over yours as you move the spatula around. Get the picture?"

"Yeah, I got it."

"Okay, now what you'll end up seeing in the final cut of the video is Jah standing at the door the entire time watch-ing you and himself essentially doing what you used to do when you were actually together. It's like he's observing a past scene in his life, in which he's actually a character." He sounded exhausted, as if that explanation sucked the wind out of his lungs.

"All right. When do we start?" I asked.

"Now."

The room swarmed with people. There was a cameraman and several bright lights that, when turned on, blinded me and made me sweat. Cliff winked at me proudly from the other side of the room.

The director sat in his chair on the other side of the kitch-en and yelled. "Quiet on the set. Everyone, please. Quiet. Jah, I need you in the doorway behind Gia. Gia, I need you at the stove. There's an egg inside of the pan. We're not going to put the fire on, but just act like you're cooking it. Jah, for this scene, remember you'll still stay in that same spot and sing the lyrics. Gia, you don't sing."

"I know that," I said, sticking up for myself.

"With that said, get in your places," he instructed.

I moved toward the stove, and Jah stood in the doorway. The music started.

It was five year ago when I met you. But it'll take an eternity to forget you. I miss holding you in my arms. Now even the memories are slipping through my fingers. You're gone.

The music was not very loud. Jah wasn't lip-synching. I could hear him quietly singing over the music. What was loud was the director's voice yelling orders to Jah and me.

I slipped into my own world. I was in my grandmother's kitchen cooking her eggs. Thinking of her was the best way for me to convey love for Jah. I stirred the eggs and smiled as I thought of her encouraging words and her gentle instruction.

It became more difficult when Jah moved closer to me. I wasn't able to think of my grandmother, and the expressions were harder to fake. Lust and love were two totally different things. Although I tried not to think of Jah during the scene, I couldn't help it. He came up close behind me, put his hands around my waist, and kissed my neck. We did the same scene with the same lyrics and the same kisses for more than two hours.

I assumed I was doing well. The director called me good, and Jah said I was easy to work with. In between takes, Jah whispered jokes into my ear that were so corny that I couldn't help but laugh. He was down to earth and made me feel comfortable — maybe even too comfortable. I had a hard time believing I was getting paid to be there.

The sunset was our cue to shoot the next scene. I went back to my trailer, and Jah went to his.

"Come on, honey child. Come to papa." Chris patted the chair. I sat down.

"Aight, for this scene," he said, taking my hair down,

"We're going for sexy, hot, fiyyyaaahhhhh!" He screeched.

"Okay, so what are you going to do with it?" I asked.

"You'll wear it down. I'm going to put a couple tracks in it to make it big, and I'm going to curl it at the ends."

"Aight, do your thing." I sat back.

I lost track of time. I started to daydream about who'd see this video and if people would actually recognize me in it. I looked in the mirror and barely recognized myself. The girl who just weeks before pulled an all-nighter in the stacks of the library at Brown University was not the girl in the mirror staring back at me. I thought of all my classmates who would see this video. I assumed, like Jahzelle's other videos, it would run on all the major music channels, and it'd start running around the time I got back on campus.

I wasn't sure I was ready for the attention. I flew happily under the radar my first semester at school. Being one of the few black students on campus, a lot of the men were intrigued by me, and the girls were curious. That didn't faze me much. I could count my friends on one hand. I thought about what Stephen would think about the video.

We met in Sociology class. I frequently got into arguments with the people there. My classmates thought that, because they read some information in a book, they understood the subject. From life experience, I knew differently. Unlike my classmates, I knew the solutions to society's problems didn't fit into a neat little box or textbook. And although we came from very different backgrounds, somehow, Stephen understood that too.

Our conversations moved from the classroom to the cafeteria to late-night study sessions in the library. I was amazed not only by the amount of things he knew but also by the way he communicated them. He let people express their points of view, but he didn't back down in presenting his.

Had I allowed it, our conversations would have gone off

campus, but they never did. Stephen often invited me to dinner, events off campus, and movies. No matter what unique idea he came up with, I shot him down.

It wasn't that I didn't like him. He was smart, funny, and good looking. He challenged me to think critically about the world around me. I always thought critically, but he challenged me to push it even further.

A lot of girls on campus threw themselves at him. I assumed that, when he wasn't trying to get me to come off campus with him, he was with someone else. But, I never saw him on campus with anyone else, and I never heard anything about him and other girls. People frequently asked us if we were a couple — a question to which I quickly answered no.

If there was even a possibility that someone could slow down my progress in accomplishing my goals, he couldn't be a priority. I was determined to keep my scholarship and graduate with honors. I was fine with having no friends in high school, and I figured it couldn't be much harder to keep that going in college. I got along with my roommate but really didn't consider her a friend, although she seemed to think differently. She'd often invite me out. I'd always decline. Come to think of it, the reason we got along so well was because she was never in the room. It was like I had a single.

But, no matter how hard I fought him, Stephen made it almost impossible *not* to be his friend. He was laid back but not a pushover. It wasn't until the last week of school that I started to let my walls down.

I was studying for finals, and somehow, he found me tucked away in my favorite studying spot — the stacks of the library. The stacks consisted of multiple floors of books. On each of those floors were rows and rows of books. It was easy to get lost up there. It was like being one letter among billions of words in millions of pages of thousands of books.

But somehow, he found me. I assumed he secretly followed me and waited a couple of hours before pretending to look for a book of 18th century European philosophers when he heard me shuffling my papers a couple of rows away. He pulled up a chair next to me, and we studied Sociology for three hours straight. Our eyes had started to blur, and we were tired. He offered to run across campus to grab us both coffee. Although I never liked coffee, I decided to see if it would help me stay awake that night. While Stephen was on the coffee run, I fell asleep on my book. I woke up to him touching the top of my head.

"Wow, your hair is really soft, Gia."

I jumped and became uncomfortable. That made him uncomfortable. He took our coffees out of the bag and attempted to change the mood by changing the subject.

"I figured you might be hungry, so I got us some fries too." He pulled the fries out of the bag.

"I am hungry, but coffee and fries, Stephen? Doesn't sound like an appealing combination."

"That's why I got you this." He pulled out a chocolate shake. I had no idea how Stephen knew it was my favorite. I never told him.

"Now, you're talking." I took the lid off the cup and took a gulp. "Mmm. Thanks, Stephen."

I licked the chocolate off my upper lip. I looked up and caught Stephen staring at me. He cleared his throat, shifted in his chair, and looked away.

"Back to studying." I attempted to ease the tension.

We spent the next twenty minutes laughing and joking, making everything in the text into a song or dirty limerick. Our study session was officially over. Our brains were the consistency of the chocolate shake I'd just devoured. At one point, we laughed so hard that coffee sprayed out through Stephen's nose.

"Stephen, you have coffee all over your upper lip," I

laughed.

He attempted to wipe it himself but kept missing small droplets above the corners of his mouth.

"You still missed a spot," I said after his third attempt. "Oh, forget it. You're useless." I used my fingers to wipe the coffee from the corner of his mouth.

He grabbed my hand, moved in close, and kissed me. Our lips touched lightly. After he pulled away, he continued to hold my hand. I smiled and let go. I pressed my lips together, secretly hoping I could still feel his. Instead, I felt something sticky.

"Gia!" Someone yelled.

I woke from my daydream. I was back in the trailer, and Alicia was applying a deep maroon lip gloss that was now all over my teeth. I felt embarrassed, now knowing where the sticky feeling was coming from, and not knowing how much of my daydream I had acted out.

"My fault, Alicia."

I was so deep in my thoughts that I didn't even notice that Chris had completed my hair and Alicia was finishing up my makeup.

"Wow," I said in response to the stranger eyeing me on the other side of the mirror.

My eyelashes magically grew. The dark shadow Alicia applied around my eyes reminded me the sun was going down, and we were about to shoot the bedroom scene. My lips were the color of dark cherries. They were so shiny that I swore I caught my reflection in them.

"You like?" she smiled.

"It's…I look…I like it." I was practically stuttering.

"Well, I'm done. You can go see Paulina now."

My hair bounced as I walked to Paulina. I couldn't help but touch it.

"Oh no, girl, you better keep those hands out of that hair!

Don't make me come over there with my curling iron!" Chris shook his curling iron at me.

"All right, all right," I snapped back.

"Okay, so here's what you'll be wearing for the next scene." Paulina pulled clothes from the racks.

She chose a black, lacy bra and a matching pair of boy shorts. I tried to hide my nerves by immediately taking off my clothes to change. My anxiety fell away with my clothes the minute I looked in the mirror. I looked sexy.

The bra made my breasts sit up perfectly. My thighs looked thin and toned. It was as if the lacy boy shorts were tailor-made for me. I felt even more confident and sexy than I did that first night at Ice.

I went to grab my robe. Alicia stopped me.

"Not yet, Gia. I need to touch up your makeup."

"Oh, okay."

Alicia had touched up my makeup in between almost every take during the shoot. I didn't protest, assuming that having on pounds of makeup was custom for a video shoot. I went to sit in her chair, and she stopped me.

"You'll need to stand for this."

She pulled out her airbrush and sprayed the top of my cleavage, my stomach, my butt cheeks, and my legs.

"You look good, but the camera hides nothing. And, you need to look *perfect* for this scene. This is what sells the music."

Sex sells, I thought to myself. But, at what cost? I convinced myself that it was fine and that it was never too late to back out. But really, I was only kidding myself. I was in too deep to look back.

After Alicia airbrushed my body, I was afraid to put on my robe out of fear of messing it all up. But, there was no way I was walking out in the cold streets of New York in a lacy bra and panties. I threw on the robe and assumed that Alicia would bring her airbrush to the set. I took a deep breath and left the trailer.

There was no chill in the air. The air was completely consumed by the chill itself. The cold was rude and obtrusive. It grabbed my ankles and ran up my bare legs, causing my skin to crawl chasing it. It was slowed by the boy shorts I was wearing but made its way through the tiny holes of the lace. It did the same to my bra, making my nipples uncomfortably hard. I crossed my arms across my chest in hopes of warming myself and preventing unwanted advances from Jah.

The director waited for me on the steps of the brownstone. He waved me inside. "Come on up, Gia. We're taping this next scene in the bedroom."

I followed him upstairs.

Sounds that I normally ignored were amplified. The stairs creaked under the weight of my feet. I heard my own breath and heartbeat. I knew the director was speaking only because his lips were moving, but I was deaf to the sounds that were coming out of his mouth. I rubbed my clammy palms together.

I walked into the bedroom and had to remind myself that this was all fake. I was playing a role. I was a character. This was not real life. I couldn't get caught up in the idea of living in a place like this, or having a boyfriend as handsome and smooth as Jah, or being this sexy with perfect hair, makeup, and clothing.

I grew up in a building that smelled of urine and cigarettes, not Christmas trees. My Prince Charming wasn't waiting outside my bedroom door to sweep my off my feet. In my world, Prince Charming was like a project building with no roaches; he just didn't exist. And I was not some exotic sex kitten who lived in a brownstone on the Upper East Side. I was a college student who was technically homeless. That's why I was here playing this role — to save enough money to get back to school for the next semester.

The bedroom was typical of the R&B music video sex scene. The bed was huge. White chiffon drapes hung from the four wooden bedposts. The sheets matched the drapes. The room was lit with candles. With all the cameras, lights, and crew buzzing around, it all felt fictitious. I liked it that way. It was another reminder that this was not reality.

I heard someone walk in behind me. It was Jahzelle. I turned around and was greeted by his killer smile.

"You ready to do this, Gia?" he asked.

I took off my robe, threw it to the side, and said, "Now, I'm ready." I was hoping that my bold action would act as a guise for my nervousness. It worked.

The smile on Jahzelle's face faded and traveled to his eyes. I was unsure why I was so surprised by the change in his demeanor. I assumed this was all just another day at the office for him. I was naïve to think he was too professional to mix business with pleasure.

He placed his hand on my shoulder and whispered in my ear, "You're a natural, Gia."

I was slightly uncomfortable but was ready to shift control back to me.

I grabbed his hand, moved it from my shoulder, held it close to my thigh, and let it brush up against my skin. I took my other hand and gently ran it down the side of his face, down his arm, and down to his hand, locking our fingers. I stepped in closer and whispered, "Tell me something I didn't already know, Jah." With that, I let go of both of his hands and walked toward the director.

"Gia!" the director exclaimed. "You look great! You sure you never did this before?"

"Not in front of a camera, I haven't."

He laughed and yelled for Jah.

"Jah, my man." He waved him over. Jah hadn't moved

from where I left him a couple of seconds ago. He walked toward us. The look on his face was a mix of excitement and frustration. My guess was that he secretly liked a challenge but forgot how it felt to have to work to get a woman's attention.

"Okay," the director started, "here's the rundown of the scene. We'll start with Jah sitting at the edge of the bed, singing. Gia walks in and stands at the corner of the bed. Gia, toss your hair, give him the bedroom eyes, and then walk over to him. Then you'll whisper in his ear and kiss his cheek. Have this go on for about thirty seconds, which is an eternity in video time. Then you'll place your hand on his shoulder, pushing him down onto the bed. Then you'll lie next to him. You'll both be on your sides. He'll start kissing you, and as soon as the audience thinks they're going to see some action, Jah grabs the pillow behind you and starts a pillow fight. You act slightly surprised, but grab a pillow and join in. We really want this scene to start off sexy. The sexual attraction has got to be there between the two of you. The last scene we shot was perfect, but now it's time to turn up the heat. During the pillow fight, we need to see that, at the end of the day, not only is there a sexual attraction, but there's a strong, unique relationship, a special bond, a friendship that Jah will regret losing later on in the story. We got it?"

We nodded our heads and took our places. Jah sat on the edge of the bed. He rested his elbows on his thighs and hung his head. When the music started, he lifted his head and softly sang over it, looking into the camera. The director yelled instructions over the music.

When the sun went down, nights were hotter than the day...

That was my cue. I walked over to the bedpost and leaned against it, facing the camera. I arched my back, tossed my hair, and crossed my arms around my stomach, gently grabbing my sides. I looked over at Jah and skated to him.

...Body so right, no word could describe...

I sat next to him and ran my hand from the top of his head down to the bottom of his chin.

I whispered in his ear, "Is this natural enough for you, Jah?" He smiled and kept singing.

I gently bit the tip of his earlobe and watched goose bumps form on his forearm. I placed my hand on one of his cheeks, pulled his head in close to mine, and kissed him on his other cheek.

...More than just a pretty face, my best friend in every way...

I stood up. Jah looked up at me. I took my hand and firmly placed it on his shoulder and pushed him onto the bed. I lay down beside him and kissed him. I didn't know what the rules were about kissing for the camera, but I assumed they were the same as kissing off camera. Because I only had one experience to draw from, I thought of the time in the stacks of the library with Stephen.

My kiss with Stephen was drastically different than my kiss with Jah. When I kissed Stephen, I felt something more than just the kiss itself. It was hard to describe. Kissing Jah was like biting into a slice of hot pizza. The anticipation of it all was exciting, but in the end, it just didn't feel all that good. I guessed that's why they called it acting. I'd later find out the kiss looked very believable on camera.

As we fell deeper into each other's lips, Jah grabbed a pillow and hit me in the head with it. I laughed, grabbed the pillow behind him, and the pillow fight was on. After about thirty seconds of the pillow fight, the director yelled "cut!"

Jah helped me up from the bed and helped me to fix my hair.

"Damn, Gia. You almost took my life with that last swing." We laughed. The director walked toward us.

"You guys must have known each other before today because *that* was amazing."

I rolled my eyes. I was tired of his BS.

"That was great, but we'll shoot it a couple more times," he said.

We all turned around at the sound of a woman's screams.

"If you knew what was good for you, you'd wait another hundred hours for me," the woman shouted.

"Oh boy," Jahzelle said as he took a seat on the bed. I stayed right where I was.

"Is this my replacement? Are ya'll serious?" She whipped her hair around and approached me. I didn't flinch.

"Baby girl you have no idea who you're messing with."

"So why don't you *show* me?" I moved in closer.

The director got in between us.

"Woah ladies easy now! We can work this out."

"We ain't working nothing out! Ya'll done really f-ed this up. I'm the biggest name in this industry! You're gonna replace me with some nobody?"

Our eyes locked and I smirked.

"This *nobody* just took your spot. So I guess that makes me a somebody. But what I still can't figure out is what that makes you."

She pushed passed the director and got in my face.

"Mark my words rookie. It'll be my feet that'll kick the pieces of your shattered dreams to the curb when this all comes crashing down."

I looked down at her feet and looked back in to her eyes.

"For now, you should probably use those feet to take your ass to the unemployment office."

The director grabbed the woman by the arm and escorted her out. Jahzelle and Cliff approached me.

"You all right Gia?" Cliff asked.

"We've already wasted too much time. Let's get back to work," I said.

We did just that. A couple more times turned into another

two hours. We wrapped at eight thirty PM.

"All right, kids. So we'll shoot the next scene two days after Christmas. We'll start at eight AM sharp so call time is at six. Don't be late. You all saw what happens when you're late."

I shook my head thinking of the confrontation that occurred a couple of hours before.

Jah walked me back to my trailer.

"So, Gia. The night is young. You have plans tonight?"

"Yeah, I do. But we can get up tomorrow. Stay here. I'll be back." I went inside the trailer and got my cell and the flyer for the party on Christmas Eve.

"Here." I handed him the flyer. I'll be there tomorrow night. I'll be at the door until two. I'll have a table and a bottle waiting for you around one thirty. I'll have my cell on me. Call me."

He took his phone from his pocket and put my number into it.

"Definitely bring some of your people through too. It's going to be a hot party."

"Yeah, but you'll be busy working," he said shyly.

"Yeah, but it's my job to make sure that VIPs like you are having a good time. Trust me. If it's wack, then I owe you. That's a promise, and I'm true to my word." I tied my hair back.

He smiled. "All right, Gia. I'm going to try to make it out. But only because you'll be there." He licked his lips.

"Okay, so I'll see you tomorrow night."

"All right, Gia." He walked to the door.

He put the flyer in his back pocket and left the trailer.

13

'TWAS THE NIGHT BEFORE CHRISTMAS

I woke to the sounds of grease popping in a frying pan. From the smell, I assumed it was bacon. I looked at my alarm clock. It was nine AM. Because it was Christmas Eve, I assumed Sam was home from work and that Dee was in the kitchen cooking for him. I still avoided Dee as much as possible. I trusted her just about as much as I trusted my mother. I got up to use the bathroom when Sam passed me in the hallway.

"Hey, Gia."

"Oh hey, Sam."

"You been busy these last couple of days, huh?" He looked over my shoulder as if the answer to his question was in my room.

I followed his gaze.

"Sorry about that, Sam. I'll clean that up today," I said, still half asleep.

"Don't even worry about all that, G. It's cool. Dee's cooking breakfast, and then we're going out to do some last-minute Christmas shopping. You want to come out with us?"

"No, I can't. I already made plans. Thanks for inviting me though."

"All right. Well, at least come have breakfast with us."

"Okay. I'll be in in a couple of minutes."

"All right, cool." He walked into the kitchen, and I went into the bathroom.

I jumped at the sight of my reflection. I was so exhausted when I came home the night before that I hadn't washed my face. My eye makeup was runny and smeared. I looked like a raccoon. My lipstick was faded and smudged all over my chin and cheeks. I took out my face wash and washcloth and washed off my mask. I didn't intend on telling anyone about my acting gig, except maybe Micah. I definitely didn't want Dee to know.

I took as long as possible in the bathroom. The less time I had to spend with Dee, the better. After dragging my feet, I finally joined Dee and Sam in the kitchen.

"Hey, Gia," Dee said nonchalantly. "Help yourself to breakfast."

"Thanks." I grabbed a plate of eggs, grits, and bacon. I sat next to Sam and gave him an envelope with $100 in it.

"Here, Sam. This is a little bit of rent. It's not much, but it's something."

He put his fork down and swallowed hard.

"Gia, you don't have to give me nothing. Like I told you before, Mich is like a brother to me. So that makes you like my lil' sister. And, I wouldn't ask my little sister for no rent money."

"I know. But it would really make me feel a lot better if you would just take it. Think of it as a Christmas present."

He looked at me as if he were uncomfortable accepting the money. He placed it in his back pocket. "You really didn't have to do that, Gia. But thanks."

"You're welcome." I bit into a piece of bacon.

"So, Gia. What are your plans for today?" Dee asked.

"Well, I'm working the Warehouse tonight. So, I'll be run-

ning around doing some last-minute things before the party."
I assumed that Dee had already planned on going to the party, but I asked anyway. "You both coming out tonight?"

"No offense, G. But that's not really my scene anymore," Sam answered.

"Girl, you know I'll be there," Dee said.

To say I wasn't excited about Dee coming to the party was an understatement, especially after what I saw her doing at Ice. I had to remind myself that, if it wasn't for her, I wouldn't have the job in the first place.

"All right, so I'll see you there. I won't be leaving from here. I'm meeting Ty at his place to talk business, and then we're going over together."

"All right. So I'll meet you there."

She sounded as if she didn't trust what I was saying. She shouldn't have. It was true that I was going to Ty's place, but it wasn't to talk business. He was having a small get-together before the party. He was going to have hors d'oeuvres, drinks, and a small number of people. I'm sure Ty wouldn't mind if Dee tagged along, but I did. So I kept my mouth shut.

After breakfast, I lay down. I considered going to my mother's apartment to collect the last of my belongings, but I decided against it. I wasn't quite ready to go over there. I knew that night would be big, so I decided to go shopping.

I wouldn't get paid from the music video until I returned to school. Unlike working for Ty, the video was not off the books, and I wasn't paid in cash. I had to wait on a check.

Between my last shopping trip, seeing Micah, and giving Sam rent money, I had about $400. I grew sad thinking of Micah. I wanted him to spend the holidays with me, not locked up in that nasty jail.

Although I really loved the dress I wore to Ice, I knew I couldn't wear it to the Warehouse. It was a guarantee that some of the same people who were at Ice on Saturday would be at the Warehouse. I decided to go shopping for a new dress in Soho.

Even after living in New York all of my life, the drastic difference among the neighborhoods still surprised me every time I left Harlem. Like Times Square, Soho was crowded. A lot of people were out doing their last-minute Christmas shopping, but there were more native New Yorkers in Soho than there were in Times Square. The streets were made of cobblestone. Women crossed them on their tiptoes to prevent their heels from getting stuck in between the stones.

Like 34th Street, Steve Madden, Aldo's, and Express were all in Soho. Armani Exchange, Prada, and Dolce & Gabana were also there.

I saw exactly what I was looking for in the window of the Kenneth Cole store. I went inside to get a closer look. I knew it was my dress the second I saw it. It was a scoopneck halter that gathered tightly around the waist and was exposed in the back. It was short and red.

"May I help you, miss?"

"Yeah, can I have this in a six?"

"Certainly."

"Oh, and you can just bring it up to the counter. I don't need to try it on." I knew it'd be the perfect fit.

I looked around to see if there was anything else I needed. I decided to look at the shoes. As I walked toward them, I noticed a small crowd forming around a man at the watch counter. I assumed he was somebody important to them, but because my shoes were important to me, I kept walking. I took a second glance at him, knowing that, once I was by the shoes, they'd have my full attention. I squinted as if that would make my vision clearer. There was something familiar about him.

I recognized the height and the build first. The muscles in his forearm flexed as he signed autographs on slips of paper and various body parts. He turned slightly, giving me a view of his profile.

It was Terrance.

I looked down and dashed for the shoe section. Terrance never called. If he wasn't interested, neither was I. Once again, the shoes became my top priority.

The color caught my eye immediately. Like the dress, they were red. My face lit up in the reflection of the patent leather. I picked up the display — a size eight. I slipped it on my foot. The heel was four and a half inches tall. It was open-toed. All toes were in full view with the exception of the pinky, which hid behind a band that spanned the whole width of the shoe and was about an inch thick. The top of my foot was exposed up to my ankle, where a strap slung back around my Achilles tendon.

They were hot. I pivoted to see how the back looked in the reflection of the mirror. I turned my foot to the side to get one last look and saw a pair of Jordans sneak up behind me.

"I think they're perfect," said a deep, masculine voice.

I turned around and was met by Terrance's face. It was a couple of inches in front of mine. I stepped back. The first and only other time I saw Terrance was inside a dark club. He definitely didn't have the dim light syndrome. The dim light syndrome occurs when you meet someone for the first time in a dark environment, like a bar or a club. They look great under the dim lights but are atrocious under brighter lights.

That wasn't the case with Terrance. He looked even better in the light that was streaming through the huge storefront windows. The only difference was that the club lights must have slimmed him down a bit, because I didn't remember him being that big. Even with my heel on, he still had a good five inches on me. Someone who never watched a day of football in her life could tell Terrance was a football player by his build alone. He reminded me of one of those bronze sculptures of a Greek god.

"Hey, Terrance," I said nonchalantly. My eyes shifted to the small crowd behind him, which hovered like mosquitoes over stagnant water. I turned back to the small mirror on the floor.

"No hug or nothing, Gia? That's messed up."

I limped over to him and gave him a pathetic excuse for a hug. I inhaled deeply. His smell was too good to ignore. He laughed, looking down at my feet.

"You gonna try the other one on?" he asked.

"I don't need to. I'm going to get them." I took one last look in the mirror. The same salesperson who helped me with the dress came over.

"Those are beautiful on you," she said.

"Yeah, I know. This is the display. Can you pull me an eight from the back and put them with my dress?" I asked, sitting down on the bench next to me, slipping off the shoe.

"Certainly." She looked Terrance up and down, her eyes full of lust. "Sir, can I help you with anything?"

"I'm good. My things are behind the counter already."

"Okay. If there is anything you need help with, let me know."

I laughed as she walked away. Terrance ignored her advances and continued talking to me.

"I've been trying to get in contact with Ty for the last three days. I think he's avoiding my calls."

"Really?" I didn't know if Terrance was telling the truth. I looked into his eyes, trying to read them. I couldn't tell if he was lying or if Ty really had been avoiding his calls. I remembered the night I left Lit with Ty. He kept hitting the ignore button on his phone. Ty almost always answered his phone because any incoming call could potentially be a business call, which could mean more money in his pocket. And, I vividly remembered telling Ty that, if Terrance called, he could give him my number.

"When did you call?"

"The better question is when *didn't* I call?" he said, putting it all on the table.

"Really?" I asked rhetorically. Either Terrance was laying it on extra thick or he was abandoning his pride. "Well, you coming through to Warehouse tonight?"

"Will you be there?" he smiled.

"Yeah." I tried to conceal my smile.

"All right. So why don't we cut out the middle man?" He took out his phone. "What's your number?"

"Come through tonight and I'll give it to you," I said.

Terrance sat down next to me.

"Wow, you're really going to embarrass me in front of all these people," he whispered. I looked behind us. The crowd grew. They were smiling, waiting patiently for Terrance to make his way over to them.

"Let me ask you something, Terrance. You get paid to make touchdowns, right?"

"Yeah," he said, unsure of what I was getting at.

"Okay, so do you do your silly little dance before or after you make the touchdown?" I asked, amused at the fact that he was unsure where I was going with this.

"After, of course."

"Okay, well, I get paid to get bodies inside of Ty's parties. Come out tonight, bring your boys, and after I'm done doing my job, we'll do our little dance. All right?"

I stood up and walked to the cash register. He followed me, blowing off the groupies.

"Yeah, I have the dress and the shoes," I said to the girl behind the counter.

"Okay, that'll be $364."

"Okay." I pulled my wallet out of my purse. Terrance came up so close behind me that I could feel his breath on my neck. He slid the sales clerk his credit card.

"I got it," he said casually.

"No," I said forcefully. "I got this." I looked directly into his eyes. We seemed to be entertaining the cashier. She smiled, took my cash, and handed me my change and the shopping bag with my dress and shoes inside.

"I'll see you tonight, Terrance." I exited the store and left Terrance to cool off with his fans.

****

I called Ty to get directions to his place. I decided then not to mention Terrance. I suspected that Ty might have been interested in me from the moment I met him. His not giving Terrance my number confirmed it. If Ty decided to act on his feelings, I'd deal with that train once it pulled into the station.

After a half hour on the A train, I was in Bed-Stuy. Ty rented an apartment inside of a brownstone on a tree-lined street. His place was beautiful. The hardwood floors that carpeted the apartment were so shiny and clean that you could eat off of them. In the living room, there were two big bay windows that watched the street. Two huge plants sat adjacent to each window. A brown leather couch sat behind a coffee table that held two books titled *A Day in the Life of Africa* and *The Black New York City*. Above a fireplace made of bricks sat a flat screen plasma TV. To the left of the living room was a desk with nothing but a Mac book and stacks of club flyers on it. The kitchen was tucked away in a corner opposite the desk. Like the kitchen on the shoot of the Jahzelle video, it had granite countertops and stainless steel appliances.

Ty greeted me with a double kiss.

"Let's talk business real quick, and then I'll introduce you to my peoples." He escorted me to an unoccupied corner.

"Okay," I said.

"So, we'll head out of here around nine. I want to get to Warehouse earlier than usual. We're expecting about four thousand people tonight. I guarantee that, by one, the street will be shut down, and by two, they'll probably shut the doors completely. I've known promoters who got shut out of their own parties before. So instead of two, we'll shut the guest list down at one tonight."

"Okay." I nodded my head.

"You look great, by the way. Usually I ask for hair to be down, but it looks good like that."

I'd decided to wear my hair up. I parted it on the side, swept my bangs over to the right side of my face, and tied it back into a high ponytail, similar to the way I wore it on the Jahzelle shoot. I'd covered the hair band with a piece of hair from the ponytail.

"Yeah, I wanted to change it up a little." I stroked my ponytail.

"And those shoes are fire." He looked down at my feet.

"Thanks." I turned my feet to the side, helping him get a better look.

"Well, I know you don't drink, but there's a full bar in the kitchen. There's some soda in there too. Just relax. You'll need to. Trust me. By the end of tonight, I won't be surprised if you're ready to quit."

"Come on, Ty. It can't be that bad."

"Hmm." He smirked. "Come see me at the end of the night, and we'll see if you say the same thing."

"All right." I walked to the kitchen to get a drink.

There was a beautiful woman who looked to be in her thirties pouring a drink.

"Hi, I'm Gia," I said.

"Hi, Gia. Nice to meet you." She put her glass down and shook my hand. "Gia, you are absolutely stunning. And those shoes!"

"Thanks." I looked down at them, knowing I made a good choice picking them out. "So, how do you know Ty?"

"Ty and I met through a mutual friend. We've known each other for about five years. How about you?"

"I work for Ty. We've known each other for about five days," I said. She laughed.

"Okay. So, what do you do?" she asked.

"I'm a freshman in college."

She nodded as if she were impressed. "What school do you go to, Gia?"

"I go to Brown University."

"I went to Dartmouth." She sounded excited.

"Really?" Now I was excited too. Finally, here was someone who understood where I was coming from. Whenever I told people where I went to school, they either assumed it was some no-name school out in the sticks or they just didn't care.

"Yeah. It's so good to meet young sisters like yourself getting a good education. What's your major?"

"I haven't decided yet."

"I understand that. I was an art major. I caught hell from my parents for making that decision. They told me I was an idiot for choosing to go to an Ivy League school to major in art and risk being jobless and broke for the rest of my life."

She had my complete attention. I was hanging on her every word. "If you don't mind my asking, what do you do?"

"I'm a museum curator for the Brooklyn Museum. I'm responsible for choosing some of the items that are displayed there. I travel to find eclectic and unique pieces. The best part about it all is that every single day of work is another day I prove my parents and everyone else who said I was a fool wrong."

We both laughed. My smile faded when I thought about my mother. She had no idea that I hadn't chosen a major yet. I could tell her I was majoring in underwater basket weaving, and it would have made no difference to her.

"I love art. I was considering majoring in it but decided against it because of similar reasons. So I took a bunch of classes first semester to see what I liked, but everything just kept coming back to art. In Psychology, the human brain was art; in Sociology, the way people interact together was art. Everything kept coming back to art."

"And it always will. Here, Gia." She pulled a business card out of her purse and handed it to me. "Give me a call. I'd love to have you as a guest at the museum. We're currently showing *the* largest collection of African-American photography. If you call me ahead of time, I can schedule a special behind-the-scenes tour for you, and we can talk more about your future career in art."

I studied her card and slid it in my purse. "Thanks. I'll definitely be giving you a call before I go back to school."

"Keep in touch, Gia. And keep your head up. You're doing well even if the people around you are telling you otherwise."

I spent the rest of the evening talking to Ty's friends. I'd been missing the variety and depth of the conversations I had with Stephen at school. It was refreshing to have that with the people at Ty's party. They were lawyers, businesswomen, teachers, and other young professionals. Part of me didn't want to leave. I could have stayed there and spoken to them the entire night. But, as the night progressed, money started to talk louder than they did, so it was time to go to work.

We arrived at the Warehouse at nine, just as Ty planned. It was nothing like Ice or Lit. It looked exactly how it sounded – like a warehouse. It was huge. There was a large, oval-shaped bar about twenty feet from the entrance. The six bartenders in the middle of it prepared for the night by placing bottles and glasses on the shelves. The dance floor was as big as a basketball court. There was a no-frills stage that looked like no more than a couple pieces of plywood hammered together with some rusty nails and a hammer. Its only decoration was a banner advertising one of New York City's premier hip-hop radio stations. There was a balcony about thirty feet up that formed a perimeter around the entire dance floor.

Ty must have seen me looking up. "There are VIP rooms up there. When it's not too crowded, they let everyone up on the balcony and have bouncers at the entrance of each room. Because it *will* be crowded tonight, only VIPs will be allowed on that level."

"All right. So, that's where I should escort Jahzelle?" I bragged.

He stopped walking and gave me a puzzled look.

"Jahzelle?" he asked.

"Yeah. I invited him to come through with his people."

"Wow, it's gonna be a star-studded event. I got a couple of artists coming out too."

"Yeah, and I bumped into Terrance earlier this afternoon. He's going to try to make it out too."

"All right, cool." His voice sounded deflated. He quickly changed the subject. "So tonight will be the same deal as Ice. We're going to let a line build outside. But tonight, there will be a lot of people out there early. We'll start letting people in earlier than usual, so the streets don't get too crazy. The cashier will have your clipboard. We're gonna be strict with the guest list tonight. Ladies whose names are on the guest list are free before midnight and twenty after. If they're not on the list, they're twenty before midnight and thirty after. For the men on the guest list, it's ten before midnight and thirty after. If they're not on the list it's thirty before midnight and forty after. Do not let anyone under twenty-one in. There'll definitely be undercover cops here tonight. So again, if you like this job and want to keep it, don't let anyone under twenty-one in."

"I got it," I said.

"All right." He walked toward the stairs to the balcony. "I'm going to introduce you to the bouncer and show you the VIP rooms. After that, I need you to get your clipboard and do your thing."

As Ty predicted, the line was around the block by midnight. I'd let a steady stream of people in since ten. My plan was to stay outside until the cops shut the doors. It looked like that was going to happen sooner rather than later.

The street was already closed off with police barricades. "Ladies and gentlemen, if you are not in line for the Warehouse, you must leave the street," the NYPD officers shouted through blow horns, riding on horseback up and down the street. From outside, you could hear the bass of the music inside. The women in line wore skimpy clothes and fidgeted to keep warm.

"What's really good with this line?" many of the women asked, obviously freezing and tired of waiting in the cold. I ignored them. I let people in when the bouncers gave me the word. I got a nod from Brock and turned toward a group of women shivering in front of me. I recognized one of them.

"Hey, Gina," she said.

"It's *Gia*," I said with an attitude. It was James's baby's momma. I couldn't remember her name, but I remembered her face. I looked down at her engagement ring and laughed out loud, remembering the note James wrote me.

"Oh, Gia. My bad, girl. You remember me, right?"

"Yeah, James's baby momma, right?"

"His *fiancé*," she said, "Janay."

"Yeah, right. Janay." I looked passed her at a group of men making their way toward the entrance. It was Jahzelle, two body guards, and some of his friends. I wasn't the only one who noticed him. The crowd went crazy. Women reached their hands out to touch him. Male groupies took out their camera phones and snapped pictures. Jahzelle shook a couple of hands and smiled when he saw me.

"Hey, Jah." We kissed on the cheek. Janay and her friends were dumbfounded.

"So, what's good, girl? You gonna be out here all night?" He put his hands around my waist and smiled. "Come inside, so I can warm you up."

I could hear Janay and her friends whispering to each other. The more he spoke, the more attracted I was to him. I don't know if it was my common sense or the wind that sobered my thinking, but I quickly remembered that we still had to work together in a couple of days. I devised a plan.

"If there's anyone who understands being a workaholic, it's you, Jah. I've seen you in action, remember?" I clutched my clipboard.

"How could I forget? Since the shoot, there's not a second that hasn't passed without the thought of you passing through my mind," he said. I looked around, hoping no one heard him mention the shoot. By the look on her face, I could tell Janay heard every single word.

"Why don't you do this," I said, backing away from him. "Go inside, have some drinks, and save me a dance. I'll be up in a little while. In the meantime, I'll send something special up for you and your boys."

"Aight, Gia. But, that something special better be you."

"All right," I said. "Go to the stairway to your right. There will be a light-skinned guy with dreads waiting to escort you upstairs."

"Okay, Gia." He leaned over and kissed me on the cheek. Brock let him in, and I radioed Ty from the walkie-talkie he'd given me earlier in the night.

"You guys'll get in in a second," I said to Janay and her friends.

"You know Jahzelle, Gia?" Janay asked.

I pretended not to hear her and walked down the line.

I was looking for a group of about five or six really beautiful women to keep Jah and his friends busy. I figured if I sent them up into the VIP room, Jah would forget about our dance, and our business relationship could remain intact.

Janay was pretty and well put together from the drug money, but I couldn't say the same about her friends. I needed pretty, well put-together women. I found them about halfway through the line.

They were a group of three. One was tall and dark-skinned. She looked like a high fashion model. The other was light-skinned, medium height, and thick. The third one was a petite Puerto Rican girl. They were stunning. They all had on stilettos, their hair was done, and they were all wearing dresses underneath their coats.

"Ladies, are ya'll three together?"

"Yeah," the one who looked like a model answered.

"But, we're waiting on a friend," the Puerto Rican one chimed in.

"Okay." I stepped in closer to them to prevent the others around from hearing me. "You can either wait on your friends or take these bracelets and go party with Jahzelle in his VIP room.

"We'll take the bracelets," they said in unison.

"That's what I thought."

I put neon-green paper bracelets around each of their wrists. I radioed Ty to let him know about the girls I was letting up. I could practically smell the look Janay gave me as I ushered them to Brock; it was that nasty. But I knew she'd keep her mouth shut because she wanted to get inside.

"Okay, ladies. Even though it's after midnight, I'll comp you for—" I was interrupted by a tap on the shoulder. It was Terrance and his smile. Again, the male groupies had their camera phones in hand, snapping pictures. The woman seemed unsure of who he was. I heard a few of them whispering to the men standing next to them, asking who Terrance was. The answer caused them to smile and reach out to Terrance.

"Hi, Terrance." I looked at Janay through my peripheral vision.

"What's good, Gia?" He gave me a hug and a kiss on the cheek.

"I got a bottle of Hennessy and Grey Goose waiting for you upstairs."

"That's cool and all but...um...when are *you* gonna be waiting for me upstairs?" he smiled. I became uncomfortable knowing that Janay was hearing me have the same conversation twice, this time with a different man.

"I guess it's true what they say. It ain't trickin' if you got it," Janay said to no one in particular. I knew she was referring to me. I had no idea what that even meant. I shifted my attention back to Terrance.

"Remember, Terrance, touchdown before the end zone dance, right?"

"Okay, I got you." Out of the corner of my eye, I saw a member of Terrance's entourage approach Janay.

"What's good, ma?" He grabbed her hand.

"I'm good," she said with a girlish grin on her face. I assumed Terrance's team wasn't all that particular with the women they chose.

"Ay yo, baby girl," one of them yelled to me. "They're coming in with us."

I looked at Terrance to get his approval.

"Yeah, it's cool." He read the question on my face. I gave Janay and her friend VIP bracelets. I radioed Ty and ushered Terrance, his friends, and Janay and her friends to Brock.

"I'll be up to give you that dance in a little, Terrance."

"All right, you better. I'll see you inside." He walked in with Brock.

I checked my watch. It was a quarter to one. The line got longer. More cops on horseback rode the street. People were starting to get desperate. They knew that, with each minute that passed, their chances of getting into the club decreased. Everyone was ready to buy a bottle until I asked them for the $400 deposit.

I was beyond frustrated when a short Latino man approached me requesting a table. "$400 deposit," I said, holding out my hand.

"Here's five. Keep the change." He slapped the cash into my hand. I looked up. His face was vaguely familiar, but the face of the woman standing behind him was all too familiar. It was Dee and the man she brought into the apartment a couple of days ago.

"Hey, Gia. Damn, looks like I created a damn monster," she said. I knew she was referring to her getting me the job and my attitude toward her and her friend.

"Hey, Dee," I said, unenthused. "My fault I didn't recognize your," I paused, "*friend*."

"Yeah, well he gave you the money. You got room for us?" Her tone was much different than it was that morning when Sam was around. We were no longer hiding our dislike for one another. I radioed Ty and escorted Dee and her friend to Brock.

The crowd was getting impatient and rowdy toward the back of the line. It was one AM, and I was about to head inside when I heard someone calling my name. I rolled my eyes, thinking there was no one else I knew who could possibly be there. I remembered Ty's words about wanting to quit by the time the party was over. I was starting to think that Ty definitely knew what he was talking about. I turned around to see who was calling me. Just when I thought it couldn't get any worse, I saw James. I sighed, thinking of the note and Janay, who I just pimped out to Terrance's friends about a half hour ago.

James was rolling deep. There had to be at least ten other men with him.

"Gia, I didn't know you worked here." He leaned in to give me a kiss on the cheek. I stepped back.

"Yeah, I do. So, what's up James? When did you get home?"

"Yesterday, and I'm ready to get it popping up in here." His friends got excited, giving each other pounds and dancing to the music in their heads.

"All right, well, it's late, and I can't let you in unless you're buying a bottle. Actually," I quickly counted the friends he had with him. "You'll have to buy two bottles. There's a five-person-to-a-bottle limit."

"I got this, Gia." He pulled out a wad of cash and started to count it right there on the street. "Here's a G. That should be enough for at least two bottles, right? And, if it's more than enough, keep the change."

Everything about James nauseated me, from the played-out cuts in his eyebrows to the ostentatious chains around his neck. His touch made my skin run rather than crawl as if it was attempting to escape his disgusting, rough hands.

"Well, I don't have any rooms left, but I have a couple of tables on the main level that are empty."

"That's cool. We'll take 'em," he said.

Because it was getting late and it looked like the cops were about to shut the doors, I decided to escort them to their table myself.

"Hey, Brock. I'm headed inside for the night. The guest list is closed. There are no more comps or discounted tickets. There are no more VIP tables either. They're all full."

"All right, Gia."

I escorted James and his friends inside. I decided not to tell him that Janay was there. He still had the right to ask for his money back, so I kept my mouth shut.

The air hit me as soon as I walked through the door. It felt heavier than the layers of makeup on my face at the video shoot. It consisted of sweat that evaporated off of a thousand dancing bodies. It was high on cigarettes and weed, and it blew in my face, giving me a contact high. I attempted to push it away with my hands. It excused itself temporarily, and like a man who just didn't get the point, was back in my face again. My nostrils flared, and my lips sealed tightly, begging me not to swallow.

No one else seemed to be bothered by it. The DJ was spinning reggae. People on the dance floor were closer than the stitches of a sweater. Women who came in with fresh wash and sets now looked like they washed their hair again, but this time in sweat. Men's T-shirts were soaked from beads of sweat that streamed down their foreheads onto their chests. There were a handful of women who had both feet off the ground, their bodies held up by the men they danced with. I looked away from the dance floor and continued to the last available VIP tables.

"Here, James. These tables are for you and your people," I screamed over the music.

"Cool." He moved to the music.

"What are you drinking?" I asked.

"Give us a bottle of Henney and a bottle of Ciroc."

"All right. You'll have a waitress in a second." As I turned to walk away, he grabbed my hand.

"Can I get a dance, Gia?" He licked his lips.

The chance of me bumping and grinding with James was like the chance of snow in July. It wasn't happening.

"I would love to James," I lied, "but I got to make this money. I know a hustler like you can understand that."

"All right, I got you, Gia. Just remember," he screamed into my ear, "keys to the Benz. They're yours when you want them."

So, should I go upstairs and ask Janay for them now or later, I thought to myself. I rolled my eyes, snatched my hand back, and looked through the crowd for the waitress. She was pushing her way through the crowd to James's table.

"Here comes your waitress. I'm out." I passed her, gave her the money for James's two tables, and shoved the extra two hundred he gave me in my bra.

I went to find Ty. Instead of it taking a minute to get to the other side of the club, it took me ten. The dance floor expanded to the area around the bar and wherever else there was a free spot on the floor. Every man I passed tried to get my attention by grabbing various parts of my body or screaming, "What's good, ma?" or "Can I get a dance?"

The floor was just as aggressive as the men. It kept grabbing onto the bottoms of my shoes with the help of chewed, discarded gum and sticky, spilled alcohol that had dried to it throughout the course of the night. There was no way I was trying to get that extra $100 by going around collecting names and email addresses. Ty could keep his money.

I finally found Ty in back of the stage. He was sitting on it, drinking a Corona. His dreads were tied back with a rubber band. He wiped his sweat with a napkin. The baby hairs around his forehead were plastered to his face.

"Hey, Ty," I screamed over the music.

"Gia. Good night. All the VIP tables are full. Good work."

"Yeah, thanks. But, you weren't playing. This place is crazy. You can forget about me going around to get names for your mailing list. You can keep that extra $100." Truth was I'd already made $300 from Dee's friend and James.

"Na, don't even worry about that. I got people out there taking care of that. Them poor girls are probably getting eaten alive out there right now."

"Yeah, it took me ten minutes to get over here from across

the dance floor."

"What time is it?" he asked.

"It's almost two."

"Aight, cool. I'll have your money for you by three thirty. You can either hang around or stop by my place tomorrow, and I'll have it for you then. If things are too crazy for you, you can head out. I have to stay to get our money."

"Yeah, it's getting a little crazy up in here. I'll probably head out in a little. I'll call you tomorrow."

"Aight, Gia."

He stood up and hugged me. He smelled like a mixture of sweat and alcohol. I assumed I did too. I left Ty and headed upstairs.

The balcony was almost as crowded as the main level. I saw more than a couple of people without VIP bracelets up there. Each VIP area was no frills just like the club. They consisted of a couple of couches and a table. There were no doors or walls to separate one table from another. Only two of the VIP rooms were guarded by bouncers. I walked over to one of them.

It was Jah's table. The girls I sent up earlier in the night were still there. All three were dancing. Two of Jah's friends danced with the light-skinned girl and the Puerto Rican, and as I predicted, Jah was dancing with the tall, dark-skinned model chick. The bouncer unchained the velvet rope to let me in.

"I'm not coming in. Just checking on my peoples," I stood on my tippy toes screaming into the bouncer's ear. In response, he nodded his head.

Jah saw me, lifted his champagne glass, smiled, and continued to dance with the girl. I winked, smiled, and kept it moving. I walked to the only other area that was guarded by a bouncer, assuming it was Terrance's table.

I spotted Dee on my way there. She wasn't at a table. I saw

her slip a small bag to a beautiful girl in a tight, gold dress. The woman slipped the bag into her bra and pulled out cash. She placed it in Dee's hand. Dee's eyes darted from side to side. She quickly walked away from the woman. I looked away from Dee out of fear that she would see me and continued to walk toward Terrance.

Janay and her friends were still there. Janay was straddled across one of Terrance's friends who, judging from his build, was a football player too. Her friends danced with his other friends. They were all so preoccupied that the only one who noticed me standing there was Terrance. He was sitting on the couch, nursing a drink and tapping his foot to the music. He stood up when he saw me and smiled. The bouncer unchained the rope. I thanked him and walked to Terrance.

"I thought you'd never make it up here, Gia."

I placed my purse on the couch and moved close to Terrance. I turned my back to him, grabbed his hands, put them around my waist, and began to move my hips. He caught on quickly and moved with me. The DJ played *Closer* by Ne-Yo.

I turned around and touched Terrance's face, still moving my hips to the beat of the song. His hands traveled lower. I smiled and pulled his hands back up to my waist. He smiled and shook his head.

"Closer," he whispered in my ear along with the lyrics to the song.

I stepped a couple of inches away and danced in front of him. He stopped dancing and watched me, moving only his head to the beat of the music. Impatiently, he pulled me back to him, and we danced until the song ended. Anxious to keep dancing, he continued to move even though the music stopped. Instead, the DJ's voice came over the speakers.

"Aight, everyone, we have a special guest for ya'll. Jahzelle is in the house."

The crowd screamed. Janay and her friends stopped dancing. They pulled their partners' hands and headed out to watch Jah's performance from the balcony. I grabbed Janay's hand as she moved toward the balcony.

"FYI, James is downstairs," I screamed in her ear.

"Girl, who?" Her breath smelled of alcohol and cigarettes. She grabbed onto me, trying to catch her balance, and busted out laughing.

"James! Jay. You know, your *baby's daddy*," I screamed. Her smile evaporated. "He's downstairs." I walked with Terrance to the balcony.

Jah was on stage. "Where my ladies at?" he screamed.

I was one of the only women who didn't scream or wave her hands in the air like a lunatic. I leaned against the balcony. Terrance was behind me with his hands around my waist.

"Ya'll wanna hear some music?" Jah continued. More screams. The music started. At the first note, most people knew it was his hit single from his second album called *Checkin' for You.*

Girl I've seen you around the hood
Let a playa know what's really good.
What's such a pretty girl like you
Doing without a man like me.
So I'll wait
Till the time is right
To ask to take you out for the night
To show you a side of the city
You ain't never seen.
I'll be checkin' for you
Come and holler at me
If you like what I got
And you like what you see
I'll be waiting right here
To show you ecstasy.

The crowd danced and sang along to the chorus. I turned to face Terrance.

"Hey, Terrance, I'm about to be out," I said.

"You read my mind 'cause I was thinking the same thing. You hungry?"

"I'm really more tired than hungry. I'm going to jump in a cab and head back uptown." I gave him a hug goodbye and walked to the stairs.

"Gia," he yelled, "let me give you a ride."

I stopped. He walked over to me. "What about your friends?" I asked.

"They're grown-ass men, Gia. They'll find their way."

I smiled, shrugged my shoulders, and walked down the stairs. He followed me. When I got downstairs, I looked toward the dance floor and saw a beer bottle fly in the air. A huge clearing formed toward the back of the club. There was a man laying on the floor and another over the top of him, pounding his fist into his face. A swarm of bouncers in black T-shirts flew to the area. Women standing around covered their heads with their arms. Men pushed their way through the crowd to join the fight. Jahzelle stopped singing. I looked back at Terrance, and he pushed me to the exit.

He leaned into me. "It's about to get real ugly up in here, Gia," he said into my ear. "Grab my hand and don't look back."

I nodded and followed him. I was beyond relieved when we made it outside. I never imagined that I would think of New York City's air as fresh. I took a deep breath and closed my eyes. The oppressive heat in the club made it feel like a comfortable sixty degrees outside. The dirty, frozen snow on the curb reminded me it wasn't.

Terrance's car was parked in the garage around the corner. He drove a Range Rover. It was black and shiny like Ty's

Infiniti. The interior was black leather. He opened the passenger-side door and helped me up. He shut the door, tipped the garage attendant, and got in.

"I know you're a big dude and all, but you can't possibly see the road with your seat back that far," I said.

He pulled his seat up and laughed. "You sure you don't want to get something to eat?"

"No. I want to go to bed." I was exhausted.

"Well, what are you doing the day after Christmas?"

"Working. Well, at night anyways."

"Okay, so I'll come get you at five. Is that cool?"

I took his phone off of the dashboard and put my number in it.

"I guess that's a yes," he said as I smiled and cracked the window. "You like Thai food?"

"I never had it."

"Aight. I know just where to take you. Don't eat too much of those Christmas dinner leftovers for lunch. Come out with an empty stomach."

I kept forgetting the next day was Christmas. To everyone else, that meant something. To me, it was just another day. Technically, it was the birth of Christ that was being celebrated, and I didn't believe in Him, so it would be hypocritical of me to celebrate. Besides, I really didn't have anyone to celebrate with. I planned on going to the jail to see Micah in the afternoon and working that evening. I assumed that, because Terrance wanted to take me out the day *after* Christmas, he *would* have someone to celebrate with.

"You don't have to worry about that. I'll be good and hungry," I said.

"What time do you need to be at work that night?" he asked.

"Ten."

"All right, so if I pick you up at five, that should give us plenty of time to have a bite to eat. I'll drop you at Ice after we're done."

"Turn here," I instructed him to turn on 116th. "Go down to Madison."

"So, five?" he asked.

"Yeah, that's cool. This is me." I unbuckled my seat belt.

"Right here? There's no apartment building here," he said, confused.

"Yeah, I live on 117th. But, you can't make a left on Madison, so I'll walk from here."

I opened the door. "I'll see you soon."

"I don't know why you just won't let me drive around the block and drop you in front of your building."

"I'll see you soon, Terrance."

I shut the door and walked to 117th. I didn't want Terrance to know where I lived. I barely knew him. Letting someone you barely know know too much about you too soon is as stupid as carrying a metal rod during a lightning storm. I turned the corner and froze like the water on the sidewalk. It was Dee. She stood at the trunk of a car about half a block from the apartment. I was too far to see what it was she was doing, but I was sure it was nothing good.

Her friend stood next to her. His head moved constantly as if he were trying to keep watch on every inch of the street. Dee's arms moved as if she were shuffling things around. She picked up her purse from the inside of the trunk and shut the door. I slid backward and peered around the corner of a closed bodega on the corner of Madison and 117th. He got back into the car, and Dee walked to the apartment. I waited about ten minutes before walking up. I hoped Dee would be in her room by the time I made it upstairs. I slipped into the building and into my room and got ready for bed.

14

CHRISTMAS DAY

slipped out of my room and shut the bathroom door quietly. As good as it smelled, I didn't plan on joining Sam and Dee for breakfast. I started the shower and thought of my plans for the day. I'd go see Micah first. I figured I'd try to stop by my mother's place for the last time to collect the rest of my belongings. I was hoping that she wouldn't be there, so I could go in and get my things without a confrontation. Then I'd come back to Sam's place and get ready for work. A knock on the door interrupted my thoughts.

"Yeah?" I screamed over the water.

"Gia, you wanna come out to Long Island with Dee and me for Christmas?"

"Thanks for inviting me, but I'm going to see Micah today and I have to work later."

"Aight, well, Merry Christmas. There's something from me and Dee for you under the tree."

"Thanks. Merry Christmas, Sam."

I wish I could have said that my gift for Sam was under the tree, but it wasn't. I figured I could always pick something up for him later. I undressed and got in the shower.

Micah wasn't his usual happy self when I got there. He had large, black bags under his eyes, and his braids were a dirty mess. I touched his hair as he sat down.

"Micah, you look like trash."

"I'm tired, G. I gotta get out of here."

I looked down and pushed his Christmas presents to him. He didn't even get to experience the excitement of opening a Christmas gift. It was already unwrapped because everything I brought in had to be checked by security first.

"It's nothing special. I just thought you could use these."

His expression changed as he looked through the socks and T-shirts I brought him.

"Nothing special? G, I couldn't think of a better gift." He leaned over the table and hugged me. Because I was used to short hugs, I let go. But he didn't. His spirit was heavier than the weight of his body. I darted my eyes to the corner of the room where an officer stood. The look on his face told me that Micah and I held onto each other for a little longer than he was comfortable with.

"Micah, let go," I whispered, trying not to embarrass him.

"I'm sorry, G." He pulled away. His eyes were wet.

"So, you'll never believe this." I changed the subject, attempting to lift his spirits.

"What's that, G?" he asked unenthused.

"You know Terrance Smits from the New York Jets?"

"Do I know him? He's one of the best receivers in the league."

"Really? Well, as soon as you get out of here, I'll introduce you to him."

"What? You know dude?" His voice picked up. I'd forgotten how much my brother loved football.

"Yeah. He's a good friend of mine," I smiled, knowing that Micah was feeling a little better.

"Gia," he hesitated, "I'm not even going to ask," he said,

shaking his head.

"I have something else to tell you," I continued, loving the fact that our conversation was putting him in a better mood.

"Oh no," he said sarcastically.

"I'm gonna be in the new Jahzelle video," I said, nervously anticipating his response.

"Yo, what?" He laughed. "That's crazy, G. I gotta be honest, though. I never pictured you as the video girl type. Matter a fact, aren't you the one who be hatin' on those chicks?"

"I know." I looked down. "I kind of just fell into the job."

"When will the video be out?" He leaned in closer.

"I'm not sure. In the next couple of weeks maybe?"

"I don't know how I feel about that, G. They might have to extend my sentence up in here if I gotta kill one of these dudes for talking sideways about how good my little sister looks in the video." He pounded his fist into his palm.

"It's not even like that. It's tasteful." I tried to convince both Micah and myself.

"Aight, G. Aight," he nodded his head yes. "So, you cool with staying at Sam's place?"

"Yeah," I said. I hated lying to my brother, but I couldn't risk telling Micah what I knew about Dee, in fear of it getting back to Sam. I couldn't risk getting kicked out of Sam's place. "Sam is a good guy. He's been wanting to come through, but he works nonstop."

"What's up with your mother?"

Why did he have to ask me that question? Now *I* was about to be in a bad mood. I desperately wanted to change the subject but didn't.

"I don't know. I haven't seen her since I got back. I was thinking about stopping by there today to grab my stuff, but I'm really not trying to bump into her."

"What do you still have at her place?" he asked.

"My high school diploma, some awards, and a couple of

my grandmother's old things," I answered.

"Yeah, you definitely need to go pick that up. That's my word, G. When I get out of here, I'm gonna get a nice place for you to come home to *anytime* you want."

"Thanks, Micah. So, you got that poem ready?"

He stood up and took the poem out of his back pocket.

"You ready?" he asked.

I nodded.

"Okay." He cleared his throat and read the poem.

"Well, son, I tell you."

I stopped him.

"Title and author, please."

"*Mother to Son* by Langston Hughes[3]."

"Okay."

He continued reading.

Well, son, I'll tell you:
Life for me ain't been no crystal stair.
It's had tacks in it,
And splinters,
And boards torn up.
And places with no carpet on the floor –
Bare.
But all the time
I'sa been a-climbing on,
And reaching landin's
And turnin' corners,
And sometimes going in the dark
Where there ain't been no light.
So boy, don't you turn back.
Don't you set down on the steps
'Cause you finds it kinder hard.
Don't you fall now –
For I'se still goin', honey,

I'se still climbing,
And life for me ain't been no crystal stair.

"Micah, that was perfect."

"Thanks, G." He smiled.

"So, what's it about?"

"A mother spittin truth to her son. She had tough times, but she never gave up. And she's telling her son to do the same. Know what I mean?"

I nodded and smiled. "Okay. This is for next time, Mich."

I handed him a piece of paper with the poem for the next week written on it.

"I wrote this one down from memory, so I hope I didn't screw it up."

"I'm sure it's fine."

"Okay, so next time?"

"Aight, G."

"I'll see you in a couple of days, Mich. Take care of yourself. I love you."

"You too. And I love you too. Stay safe."

"Merry Christmas, Micah."

"Merry Christmas." We hugged, and I headed for the exit.

I got off the D train at 155th. It was unusually quiet outside. But as always, the hustlers were on their corners. Even on Christmas, the junkies needed their highs. Everyone else was inside celebrating the holiday with their families. I took a deep breath and walked to the building, hoping and praying that my mother was out looking for a hit.

I didn't bother knocking. I took the risk of letting myself in. As usual, the apartment was filthy. There was trash on the floor, and it smelled of old beer. I didn't hear anyone, so I assumed no one was there and went to my room.

Everything was torn apart. My mattress was flipped over, and all my dresser draws had been pulled out. I wasn't surprised. This scene was all too familiar. Whenever my mother was low on cash and desperate to get high, which was all the time, she'd tear up the place looking for loose change under couch cushions, in pants pockets, underneath mattresses, and in my dressers. I stepped over the mess to get to my closet. The shoebox that held the belongings I came for was on the floor. The pictures and papers that were inside were tossed all over my closet floor like rice after a wedding.

I knelt and placed the pictures and papers back into the box. Most of the pictures were of me and my grandmother when I was a child. There was one that held my gaze.

I was about five years old sitting on my grandmother's lap in her living room. There was a Christmas tree beside us. I wore a beautiful, ruffled dress with white tights and shiny black shoes. My grandmother wore her Sunday best as well. Her arms wrapped around my waist like a beautiful ribbon on a very special gift. Judging from the expression on my face, she must have been tickling me.

A nervous laugh escaped my lips, and I felt a warm liquid trickle down my left cheek. I quickly wiped it away, shoved the picture in the box, and began to do the same with the others on the floor. I also placed my high school diploma into the box along with the honors certificates I received every year from the time I was in kindergarten to the time I was a senior in high school.

I looked around the room to see if there was anything else I wanted to take with me. It was now or never. Collecting the last of my things meant I'd never have to return to this place.

There was one more thing I needed.

I went into the bathroom and opened the lid on the back of the toilet. I was excited to see that it was still there. It was a small jewelry box with a black ballerina on the lid. My grandmother had given it to me on my sixth birthday. I heard her voice as if she were standing right there beside me.

"Gia, you're getting older now, which means I can trust you to have more responsibility with nicer things. Now, you need to be very careful with this. It's made of ceramic, which means it can break."

She wound the side of the jewelry box, and the ballerina began to spin and music played. I smiled. Holding the sides of my dress, I spun around as the ballerina did.

I kept the box at my grandmother's apartment until she passed. Out of fear that my mother would try to sell it, as she did with so many of my other toys, I hid it in the back of the toilet. I secretly took it out and wiped it down everyday.

Because I took public transportation to school, I packed as light as possible and didn't take the jewelry box with me. After being stowed in the toilet so long, it was rusty and no longer played music. The ballerina just sat there lifelessly. Her once-white tutu was now the color of old pipes, and the beautiful smile that she once wore had flushed away a long time ago.

I picked it up, shook it, and wiped it down with a piece of toilet paper. The toilet paper wasn't very absorbent and broke apart and clumped up on various parts of the box. I left the toilet lid on the floor, knowing that no one would even notice that anything was any different. I placed the jewelry box in the shoebox with the rest of my things. I left the apartment and locked the door behind me.

"That you, Tangia?" I rolled my eyes, recognizing the voice immediately.

"Hey, Ms. Frazier," I said without looking in her direction.

There was never a moment that Ms. Frazier didn't have her ear to the door. She lived next door to me for as long as I could remember. Somehow, she knew everyone's business, but when it came to helping someone out when their business was bad, she turned a blind eye.

"Tangia, the ambulance came and got your mama the other night. Think they took her over to 168th."

I remembered my mother was pregnant. My stomach turned thinking about another innocent child being raised by that woman. I wasn't sure what to think or say.

"Yeah, Ms. Frazier I know," I lied. "Thanks for your concern." I walked away. Did my mother go into labor? Was it possible she overdosed and lost the baby? If she did overdose, there was still a good chance that the baby could survive. I should have been born dead. My mother did a whole lot more than just crack when she was pregnant with me.

I decided to block the image of my baby brother or sister from my brain. Things were different than they were back when I was born. Social workers were bound to take the baby away from her, and it would be easier for a baby to be adopted than an older child. It could have a better life than I did.

"Gia!" Someone shouted at me as I walked outside.

I rolled my eyes, sighed, and said to myself, "This is exactly why I hate coming out here." I turned around and saw James.

"Ay, yo, Gia," he said, running over to me. His breathing was heavy when he reached me.

"Yo, that party was off the hook last night, girl."

"Yeah." I kept walking.

"Where you going?"

"Home."

"Oh, you don't stay here?"

"I haven't stayed here since I left for school."

"School girl. Sexy and smart. Mmm. Just like I like em." He licked his lips and I kept walking.

"Damn, girl. You gonna have me chase you all up and down these streets?" he asked.

"I gotta go."

"Well, at least let me give you a ride?"

"Nah, I'm good." He took his car keys out of his pocket

and disarmed the alarm. I saw the lights blink on Janay's baby blue Benz, which was parked across the street.

"Remember those keys I promised you? They're yours if you want em." He dangled them in my face.

"I thought this was your baby momma's car?" I asked.

"Please. It's a wrap for her. She stayed creeping."

"And you don't?" I asked. He didn't answer. "That's what I thought." I turned around and walked toward the train.

"You got my number, girl. Anytime you're ready."

I shook my head and walked underground.

It was only five when I got back to Sam's place. I didn't have to be at Lit until 10. It didn't surprise me that people partied on Christmas night. Most people had off the day after Christmas, which meant the night before was a perfect night to party, even if it *was* Christmas.

I placed the things I'd collected from my mother's apartment into the closet in my bedroom. I went into the hallway closet to get a throw blanket to keep me warm while I watched TV. My eyes were drawn to a large, black duffel bag that sat on the closet floor. I remembered the bag Dee's friend brought into the apartment a couple of days before. I bent down and unzipped it. My eyes widened. The bag was full of tiny, zip-locked bags of cocaine.

It didn't surprise me that Dee was selling drugs. I saw her do it the previous night at the Warehouse. What *did* surprise me was that she kept it in Sam's apartment. I closed the bag and grabbed a blanket from the shelf at the top of the closet.

I went into the kitchen and took a bag of microwavable popcorn out of the cabinet. I unwrapped the cellophane and put the bag into the microwave. While waiting for the popcorn, I walked to the fridge to pour a glass of cranberry juice. I thought about my dilemma with Dee as I poured. I needed to talk to Sam about what was going on. Sam was always so busy working that he probably had no idea that he had over a $100,000 worth of coke right underneath his nose. Dee was not only putting herself in danger, but she was also putting the man who was supporting her in danger. More importantly, she was jeopardizing the roof that was currently over my head. I'd talk to Sam as soon as Dee wasn't around.

As the popping of the popcorn slowed, I knew it was ready. I grabbed it and made my way into the living room.

"Merry Christmas." I lifted my glass in the air as if I were toasting to it.

I looked underneath the tree and saw the gift Sam left for me. I reached down and opened the card first.

Merry Christmas, Little Sis. Hope you like the gift. You always have your head in a book. Hope you haven't read this one already.

I smiled and unwrapped it. It was the novel *How the Garcia Girls Lost Their Accents* by Julia Alvarez. I smiled, thinking that Sam must have seen my book of poetry by the same author laying around. I read the synopsis on the back of the book, put it down next to me, and turned on the Independent Film Channel.

The Rabbit-Proof Fence was on. It was the perfect Christmas present. It was a story about three young Aborigine girls from Australia who were kidnapped from their homes. They risked their lives by escaping the camp and walking through the unpredictably dangerous Australian Outback, all to return home to the families they loved. The movie ends with a written narrative explaining that, after surviving their journey and returning home, they were captured again, and again made the journey back home.

I set the alarm on my cell phone for eight thirty PM, fought sleep, but eventually dozed off.

15

FIRST DATE

Christmas night at Lit was busy, but it was nowhere near as bad as Christmas Eve at the Warehouse. The crowd was much more laid back. Like the last time I worked Lit, I left the club around two AM, when the guest list closed. Leaving early enabled me to get a good night's sleep. I woke up around ten and spent the day at Sam's place getting ready for my date with Terrance.

Sam worked the entire day, and Dee was in and out of the apartment. I locked myself in my room to avoid her.

I met Terrance at the same corner where he dropped me off two nights before. He stepped out of the car, ran around to the passenger side, and opened it for me.

"Thanks." I stepped inside. The car smelled of the same cologne Terrance wore the day I saw him at the Kenneth Cole store downtown. He smelled great and looked clean. He had a fresh cut, and from the new, black leather shoes on his feet to his dark blue jeans and designer graphic T-shirt, there was no denying he looked good.

"You look good, Gia," he said.

"Thanks." I wore the same sweater dress and boots I wore

the day of the video shoot. "So, where you taking me?"

"We're going to Williamsburg." He drove to the FDR Drive.

"Brooklyn?" I asked, confused. "There are a million and one restaurants right here in Manhattan. Why are we going all the way out to Williamsburg?"

"You'll see. It's one of my favorite restaurants and will be yours too in a couple of hours," he said confidently.

"All right." I was unconvinced.

"So, Gia. You grew up in Harlem?"

"Yeah. Born and raised. How about you? Where'd you grow up?"

"I grew up on the West Coast. Inglewood, California. You ever been out to the west coast?" he asked.

"No." Truth was, the first time I left New York was when I left for Rhode Island to go to school. I had a strong desire to see other places, especially since I didn't plan on returning to New York after I graduated. "Do you miss it?" I asked him.

"Sometimes. New York is different, but I appreciate how real people are out here. They'll let you know what's up straight up. That's what attracted me to you." He took his eyes off the road and looked at me.

His comment reminded me of how I first met Terrance. The truth was that he was interested after seeing me for less than a second outside of the club. He showed up at the Warehouse, like I requested, and I had to follow through on my promise by giving him my number. I worried that I'd led him on by dancing with him the way I did. I actually surprised myself when we danced that night. I wasn't expecting to do it, but I needed some sort of release for the sexual tension that built up during the Jahzelle video.

"Oh, really?"

"Yeah, and it didn't hurt that you look the way you do," he said as if he were delivering lines written on a cue card. Not wanting to hear any more, I turned up the music.

Terrance was right about at least one thing. The restaurant was beautiful. It was dimly lit. A small disco ball shot a rainbow of colors onto the walls. There was loud house music playing. In the middle of the restaurant stood a Buddhist goddess, whose reflection was cast into a small, rectangular pool in front of her.

People sat at the bar in the front end of the restaurant, drinking and waiting for tables to free up. We weren't forced to wait for a table. One was ready as soon as Terrance gave his name to the hostess.

"Your server will be with you shortly," the hostess said, seating us at a table adjacent to the pool.

"Nice place, right?" He was obviously proud of his choice of restaurant.

"Yeah, it's cool." I casually looked through the menu.

"What do you want to drink?" He leaned in close so as not to shout over the music.

"I'm good with a ginger ale."

"You don't drink?" he asked.

I hung my head and rolled my eyes. I took a deep breath. "Yeah, I do. I just don't drink alcohol.

"Why not?"

Our conversation was interrupted by the server. "Can I start you off with drinks?"

"Two pomegranate martinis please."

"Okay." The waiter put our drink orders into an electronic keypad.

I couldn't believe him. After I had just finished telling this imbecile that I didn't drink alcohol, he orders me a martini. I considered agreeing to the drink just to throw it in his face but decided against that.

"Um, no. I'll have a ginger ale," I said to the waiter.

"Okay." He looked slightly frustrated, updating the information in his keypad.

"Ahh, come on, Gia. Live a little."

"I told you I don't drink." *And if I did*, I thought to myself, *I'd order something stronger than a pomegranate martini.* To me, a man ordering any kind of drink with a fruit in it was sweeter than the drink itself.

"Why not?" He pressed on.

I ignored him and asked the waiter about the pad thai. Terrance looked up at me and laughed.

I didn't.

He looked back down at his menu, "I usually get the Rama the King."

Again, I ignored him. "So, yeah, I'll have the pad thai," I said to the waiter.

"Yeah, and you already know what it is. Rama the King for *the king.*"

"Is he really serious?" I said under my breath.

"What was that Gia?"

"Nothing." I felt like I was in a nightmare I couldn't wake up from. I decided to make small talk to ease the tension I was feeling and to make the date go quicker. "So, how did you become a football player?"

"Well, I started playing when I was six. Was an all-star in high school, got a scholarship for college, and was drafted to the NFL after my sophomore year." He grinned.

"So, you never finished college?"

"Hell no. Do you know how much money I make, Gia?" he laughed.

"No. But I do know that a football player's career is a short one. I also know a college degree is stronger than an injured knee."

"Well, you obviously don't know how much money I make," he said, obviously annoyed.

With that said, I knew it was going to be a long night.

I looked up at who I thought was the waiter standing at

the end of our table. Instead, it was a woman holding a marker and staring at Terrance.

"You're Terrance Smits from the Jets, right?" she asked.

"Yeah, that's me," he smiled and stared at the woman's cleavage. It was impossible *not* to stare.

"Oh, my God! I'm such a big fan. Can I have your autograph, please?" she giggled and fidgeted like a child.

"No doubt. Terrance loves the fans," he said. The woman handed him the marker. He removed the cap and looked confused.

"You got a piece of paper?" he asked.

I couldn't believe what she did next. The woman leaned on the table and pushed her breasts together.

"Sign right here," she said, making eyes at Terrance.

He signed her chest and said, "Ahhh, another hard day at the office."

"Thanks," she said and walked away. She didn't look at me once. And while she was at the table, neither did Terrance.

"I love my job - minus the male groupies. Can't deal with all that homo stuff. You feel me G?"

I didn't respond.

The waiter came back with our drinks. "Excuse me, where's the restroom?" I asked the waiter.

"Straight back."

"Thanks. Excuse me."

"No doubt, G." I grabbed my purse and coat and headed for the restroom. Three women were ahead of me in line. I peeked back to the table. Terrance was looking down at his phone. I threw on my coat and walked to the exit on the opposite side of the restaurant.

"Excuse me," I said to a couple walking down the street. "Where's the nearest train?"

"The L train on Bedford Avenue. It's two blocks down."

"Thanks." I took off in the direction of the train.

After trying to salvage the conversation once unsuccessfully and being blatantly disrespected by Terrance twice in less than twenty minutes, there was no question in my mind. I was done with him.

16

TROUBLE IN THE CLUB

Ty stressed how big the party would be that night, but what he failed to mention was that *Upscale Urban Magazine* was holding a model search at Ice. Every girl and her sister turned out. Looking at the women in line, ninety percent of them had no chance of becoming models, but I guess everyone has the right to dream.

There was no need for me to hold up the women's line that night. The women easily outnumbered the men. Janay and her same group of friends were in line. I walked to the middle of the line where they were standing and handed them comp passes. I was uncomfortable with how much Janay knew about me and didn't want to risk a repeat of what happened in line at the Warehouse.

They snatched the tickets from my hand without thanking me.

"Cousin, my ass," I overheard one of them say as they walked to the front of the line. I had no idea what she was talking about, but I knew she was referring to me by the evil look she shot at me.

The representatives from *Upscale Urban Magazine* announced the winner of the search around one. After the announcement was made, a lot of the women left.

"It's a wrap for the night," Ty said. "You can head out if you want. I have to stick around to get our money. If you want to stick around, I can give you a ride back uptown."

I looked at my watch. It was one thirty. Ty probably wouldn't leave until four, and I had to be up early for the next part of the video shoot.

"Thanks, Ty, but I have to be up early tomorrow. I'm going to head out."

"All right," he hugged me and gave me a kiss on the cheek. "I'll see you tomorrow."

"Okay," I said.

I walked to the bathroom. The bathroom attendant had left for the night, and it was filthy. The doors of all the stalls were closed, looking as if they were occupied. I squatted down low to look for feet underneath the doors. There were none. All the stalls were empty.

I attempted to stand back up. Instead, I was pushed to the floor and felt a pain in my back.

"I'll give you the keys to the Benz, you slut bitch!"

I looked up. Janay and her two friends towered over me like skyscrapers. I thought of her words and remembered James's proposition.

I looked back down at the floor I was laying on. I tried to avoid the puddle of liquid I was laying next to. I placed all my weight on my hands, attempting to push myself up.

Seeing that I was struggling, one of Janay's friends said, "You need some help up?"

Not waiting for my answer, she grabbed my hair and dragged me across the wet floor as if I were a mop she was using to clean it. It smelled of urine and alcohol and was muddy.

After dragging me to the other end of the bathroom, she let go of my hair. I covered my face and drew my knees in toward my chest. Laying in the fetal position, I attempted to protect myself, but it didn't work. One of them kicked me in the ribs, knocking the wind out of me and leaving me gasping. I grabbed my sides as if that would help to ease the pain, but it didn't.

I got kicked again, this time in my chest.

"Ahhh!" I screamed in agony. I placed my hands back over my face, uncomfortable with how close the previous kick came to it. I quickly regretted that decision. Someone kicked me in the stomach. The force of the kick made me vomit on the nasty tile floor.

"Nasty bitch!" one of them screamed at me, pushing the ball of her foot into my cheek, causing the whole left side of my face to become submerged in my own vomit.

"Stand her up," Janay instructed her friends.

They pulled me off of the ground. My bruised body was limp and my head hung like a withering flower. It felt as if my arms would disconnect from their sockets. I was in such intense pain that I was unable to stand on my own two feet.

I struggled to lift my head. I caught a glimpse of Janay's face. It was the color of fire. She removed the rings from her fingers. I wiggled, trying to break free, anticipating what was coming.

"Jahzelle and football players ain't enough for you, huh? You need my man too? Ho."

She balled up her fingers and cocked back her fist. She punched me in the face twice. After the second punch, I fell to the floor, and the room went black.

The feeling of cold water on my face awakened me. My vision was blurred. As my eyes slowly adjusted to the light, I covered my face and backed up in fear as several large silhouettes hovered over me. I thought Janay and her friends were ready for round two.

"Gia, it's okay. It's me, Ty. What happened?" he asked.

I moved my hands away from my face and looked up at him. I wiped my nose and looked at my finger. It was coated with blood. I tried to get up.

"Ahhh!" I clutched my sides.

"Gia, who did this to you?"

"I don't know," I lied. Tears burned the cuts on my face.

"How many fingers am I holding up, G?" Ty asked.

"Two."

He nodded. I assumed I guessed right.

"Should I call an ambulance?" one of the bouncers asked.

"Nah, I think she's all right." Ty wiped my nose with a wet paper towel. I wiped the tears from my eyes and the corners of my mouth with the back of my hand.

"You're gonna be fine," Ty assured me. He picked me up and hugged me. I rested my head on his shoulder and felt safe in his arms.

"I'm gonna get her cleaned up," he told the bouncers. They formed a circle around us and led us out through one of the back entrances.

Ty placed me in the passenger seat of his car. I leaned my head against the window.

I winced at the pain of the pressure of my head against the window. Ty leaned over and reclined my seat.

"Thanks, Ty," I whispered.

I lay there silently and watched the buildings streak by. My throat burned as I held back tears. My thoughts raced. How did I get so caught up?

Even thinking hurt too much. The lights of the Brooklyn Bridge were menacing. I shut my eyes and dozed off.

I woke up when Ty lifted me out of the car. He carried me upstairs to his apartment and into his bathroom.

"Can you stand, Gia?" he asked.

"Yeah," I answered.

He put me down. I was able to stand but not without pain

shooting through every muscle of my body. He flipped on the light. I was horrified at the person staring back at me in the mirror.

I had dried remnants of the own vomit on my cheeks. Dried blood crusted in my nostrils. My right eye was an awful purple, and my lips were cut and swollen.

Ty pulled out a washcloth from the closet. He wet it with warm water and began to clean the vomit off my cheek. I stared at him in the reflection of the mirror. He was beautiful. I snapped out of an oncoming daydream, took the washcloth from him, and finished what he started.

"Thanks, Ty. I got it." I wiped my face.

"Gia, what happened in there?" he asked.

"It's a long story, Ty."

He sat down on the edge of the tub. "I'm not going anywhere."

I took a deep breath and started to explain. "Well, there's this guy from around my way. He kept trying to get at me. I wasn't interested, but I guess his baby's momma thought I was, and she and her friends attacked me."

Scenes of my encounters with James and Janay flashed in my head — from the first time I saw him in the jail, to the first ride she gave me back to the Polo Grounds, to the note he wrote me, and our encounter on Christmas Day.

"Damn, G. After you finish cleaning up, make yourself comfortable. There are towels and washcloths in the closet. There's soap and a new toothbrush in the medicine cabinet. I'll set a pair of sweats and a hoodie out for you on my bed. I'll sleep on the couch."

"Thanks, Ty."

"No problem." He made his way toward the bathroom door.

I put down the washcloth, undressed, and started the shower.

17

WHEN IT RAINS...

I slept for two hours. Call time was at six AM, and I intended to be on time, regardless of what happened the night before. I left the sweats on and found a hat in Ty's closet to help to cover my face. I let myself out of the apartment while Ty was still asleep.

I made it to the set on time. We were shooting at Club Tyranny on the west side. Cliff was standing outside the entrance.

"Is that you, Gia?" he asked, trying to look under the brim of my hat.

"Yeah." I looked down.

"I didn't recognize you with the hat. Well, anyway, I wanted to remind you to stop over to my office in the next couple of days, so you can fill out the paperwork and get paid."

"Okay," I said softly and motioned for the door handle.

"Wait. Are you okay?" He lifted my chin with his hand. His eyes widened, and he stepped back. "What the hell happened to you?" he asked, grimacing.

"It's nothing."

"Have you looked at yourself in the mirror this morning?"

I did. I looked worse than I had the night before. My eyes were unevenly swollen, and my lips were puffy and horrid.

"I got jumped last night. But it's nothing a little makeup can't fix." I tried to convince both Cliff and myself.

"You don't actually think you're going to go on set looking like that, do you?" he asked.

"Watch me." I walked inside.

The director stood a few feet away from the entrance. He spotted me as soon as I walked in.

"Our star is here," he said.

I smiled, thinking everything would be all right. He approached me and his smile vanished.

"What the hell happened to your face?" he shouted. Everyone within a ten-foot radius turned toward us.

"It's a long story. Where's hair and makeup?"

I heard someone come through the door behind me. I turned around and saw Jahzelle.

"What the hell?" he asked.

"I can't shoot you looking like this. I can't shoot her like this," the director shouted to no one in particular. "Alicia!" he yelled, storming off.

"What happened to you, girl?" Jahzelle asked with a disgusted look on his face.

"I got jumped," I whispered.

"Damn." He shook his head and walked away.

I lifted my chin and followed Jahzelle, unwilling to feel sorry for myself. The director stopped me with a glare and a hand. He stood with Alicia and examined me. A spotlight shone in my face. I shut my eyes and turned away, avoiding the painful light. The director pushed my head back in the direction of the spotlight.

"Alicia, can you do anything with this face?" Alicia put her hand on my chin.

"No amount of makeup would cover this up," she said

coldly. I pushed her hand off of my face and stormed out.

"That's show business," he shouted as I walked away.

"Gia!" Cliff yelled for me as I walked out. I ignored him. I was going home.

"Hey rookie."

I recognized the voice immediately. It was the woman from the shoot. I looked up at her. She began to laugh.

"I hate when I'm right," she said. "Wait a second. What's that?" She looked down at the curb and I followed her gaze. There was nothing there.

"Let me just kick this to the side." She kicked a couple of small pebbles off the side of the curb. I hung my head and walked toward the train.

"I told you it would all come crashing down," she yelled down the street. I didn't look back.

When I stepped off the train at 116th and Lenox, five cop cars sped off down the street with sirens blaring. I covered my ears with my hands. My headache amplified every sound and light. The intensity of the cop cars was insanely irritating.

I walked to 117th toward Sam's apartment. I felt nauseated as I neared the apartment. I stopped at the corner of 117th and Madison. The same cop cars I saw coming from the train station were now in front of Sam's building. Police crouched behind their cruisers with guns drawn. They were dressed in all black. One held a large bar that I'd seen used before in the Polo Grounds. It was used to pound a door in. Some held plastic shields to cover their chests and faces. The one leading the group nodded his head and pointed his finger. The others followed his cue and advanced up the stairs.

I knew they were heading for Sam's apartment.

I waited. Dee was dragged out in handcuffs ten minutes later. She was in her nightgown and there was a scarf on her head. It looked like they had literally dragged her out of bed. She was kicking her feet and trying to escape the grasp of the two officers who held her. Two officers carrying two large duffel bags walked out behind her.

Sam never came out. I looked down at my watch. It was seven AM. He was already at work.

A news van sped around the corner. A reporter and a cameraman from Channel 7 News jumped out. The reporter smoothed out her hair and started to speak to the camera.

I called Sam.

"This is Sam. Leave a message after the beep."

"Sam, it's Gia. Call my cell as soon as you get this message. It's an emergency."

I didn't know where to go or what to do. There was no way I was going anywhere near the apartment. Dee had over $100,000 worth of cocaine in there. She was going down and getting locked up for a long time. Because Sam and I lived in the apartment, we could go down with her, and Dee couldn't be trusted. Something told me she was the snitching type. She'd be quick to drop names, even innocent ones, to save her own ass.

A crowd started to form. People stopped walking to see what was going on. People stood on their stoops and watched Dee being shoved into the cop car. Some even snapped photos with camera phones.

It was time for me to go.

I went to the diner on 116th and Park. Luckily, I had all my money on me. The night I found out Dee was a coke fiend, I started carrying all my money on me every day. Unfortunately, I only had $500 to my name. Ty owed me about $200 from the night before. My books would cost about $400, and I needed to make sure that wasn't spent before I got back to school.

"Can I help you?" the waitress asked. When I looked up from the menu, she quickly looked back down at her pad to prevent herself from staring at the bruises on my face.

"Yeah. Can I have a glass of orange juice, a separate glass of ice, and bacon, egg, and cheese on a roll? Oh, and a lot of napkins." I handed her the menu.

"Okay." She grabbed the menu and walked away.

Sitting and waiting for my food gave me time to process the things that had happened over the past twenty-four hours. I assumed Janay saw me talking to James on Christmas Day. It made sense that he would spend Christmas with his child. Her car was parked right outside of the building. If she was watching us talk outside, she probably didn't need to say anything to me then. She knew I worked the clubs. It was the perfect opportunity for her to get her crew together, so I wouldn't have a fair shot defending myself.

"Coward," I whispered to myself.

The waitress brought me my orange juice, ice, and napkins.

"Thanks," I took a sip of the orange juice and winced. The acidity burned the cuts on my lips. I took the glass of ice and placed it against my cheek. It burned, but I forced myself to leave it there. My cheek had been throbbing since I woke up.

How stupid could Dee have been? She was selling and doing drugs inside of nightclubs. She was stashing them in her apartment, and she let that man know where she lived. She'd be the first one he snitched on.

My phone rang. I looked at the caller ID. It was Sam.

"Sam!"

"Gia, what's up? Are you okay?" he shouted over what sounded like a jackhammer in the background.

"No. Meet me at the diner on 116th and Park."

"Gia, I can't. I'm at work. What's wrong?" he asked.

"You need to leave work now! They're probably on their way there now," I screamed into the phone, drawing stares from people in the restaurant.

"Who? What the hell are you talking about?"

"The cops. They raided your apartment. They arrested Dee." I lowered my voice.

"What!"

"I was going to tell you, Sam. Dee's been selling drugs." I wished I had told him sooner.

"Where did you say you were?"

"The diner on the corner of 116th and Park."

"Aight, I'll be right there. Don't leave."

"I won't."

He hung up as my food arrived. I could only take small, slow bites. I ate quietly and Sam arrived as I took the last bite of my sandwich. He sat down across from me.

"Gia, what the hell happened to your face?"

"I got jumped. But, that's not why I called you down here."

"You got jumped? By who?"

"No one important. Sam, listen to me." I stopped, looked around the restaurant, and lowered my voice to a whisper. "The cops raided your apartment. Dee had duffel bags full of cocaine stashed there. They arrested her and will probably be looking for you. I saw them arrest her. I didn't go near the building. I turned around and immediately came over here."

He placed his face in his hands and rubbed his temples hard. He slammed his fist on the table. The glasses and silverware shook from the force of his fist. Everyone in the diner looked at us.

"All right, Gia. Whatever you do, *do not* go back to the apartment. You hear me? You're guilty by association right now. I'm going to head over to the precinct and clear my name. That might take all night. I need to call my lawyer." He took out his cell and pressed a button.

"It's Sam. My girl just got arrested for drug possession, and I think she was selling out of my apartment." He paused. "Yeah." Another pause. "Yeah, okay. I can meet you there in twenty minutes. Aight, bye." He hung up and looked back at me. "Gia, do you have someplace you can stay tonight?"

"Yeah," I lied, not wanting Sam to worry about finding me a place.

"Aight, so here's the deal. I'm going to meet my lawyer downtown. Then I'm heading over to the precinct with him. There's a good chance I'll be over there all night. Keep your cell on. I'll call you when it's safe for you to get back into the apartment."

"Okay," I said.

He stood up and walked out.

I wasn't sure where to go. I looked down at the clothes I was wearing. I had on Ty's oversized sweat suit and my heels. I looked ridiculous.

I didn't even have my coat. Ty carried me out of the club so quickly the previous night that he didn't get my coat from the coat check. I considered going back to my mother's apartment. I didn't have any clothes there, but at least I could take a shower and get cleaned up. And, if what Ms. Frazier said was true, maybe I'd have the place to myself and stay there for the night.

I looked out the window. There was a mom-and-pop clothing store across the street. I decided to go over and buy a pair of jeans, a long-sleeve T-shirt, and a lightweight jacket. I'd risk the cold temporarily. I planned on getting my jacket back that night before I went to work, or so I thought.

18

BACK TO THE BRONX

I went back to my mother's place to take a shower. I unlocked the door, turning the key slowly. The place looked the same as it did the day before and every other day before that — filthy. I walked to the bathroom and started the shower.

There were no clean towels. I turned Ty's sweatshirt inside out and dried myself with it. I went to my room to get dressed. I heard voices coming from the living room. I dressed quickly, threw Ty's clothes in a shopping bag, and headed for the door.

Three men sat on the living room couch. I recognized one of them. It was the man who was there the day I returned from school. He was the first to look over at me.

"Hey, girl," he said in a raspy voice as if he'd known me for years.

"Who dat?" one of the other men asked.

"You can't tell by looking at her face. That's Kizzy's daughter, Tangia," he responded.

"Resemblance? That girl fine! And Kizzy is, well...." He cleared his throat.

"Go to hell," I yelled at him. Anyone who knew my mother before the drugs knew she was a beautiful woman. But anyone meeting her now would never know it.

"When's the last time you saw my mother?" I asked the man I recognized.

"'Bout a couple of days ago. She be back any day now. She does this sometime. Up and leave for a couple of days and come back when she good and ready. Figured I'd watch over the place for her." He took out a small ziplocked baggie of cocaine and started lining it up on the table.

"I'm out." I wasn't even going to put up a fight. My mother stopped caring about herself, me, and that apartment a long time ago. Now it was my turn to not give a damn.

I was running out of options for places I could spend the night. I could walk a couple of buildings over and stay with James if I didn't fear for my life. I felt sick thinking about sharing a bed with him.

I could call Terrance, but I pretty much burned that bridge when I left him at the restaurant. I knew I could spend the night at Ty's place, and it was comfortable and quiet. Ty made me feel safe. And the more I got to know him, the more attracted I was to him. I wondered how much safer I'd feel if he slept in the bed with me. I smiled, not knowing where those thoughts were coming from. They excited me in a strange way.

I called Ty. There was no answer. I decided to take the train out to Brooklyn and try my luck showing up unannounced.

One of Ty's neighbors was coming out of the building, so I didn't need to ring the bell to be buzzed in. I got excited when I heard music playing. It sounded like John Legend. I smiled, thinking about our similar tastes in music. My heart began to race. I smoothed out my hair and took a deep breath.

I rang the bell twice. There was no answer, so I knocked.

I heard fast footsteps shuffle to the front door. Ty opened the door. I smiled, feeling more attracted to him than ever. His shirt was off, and his body was amazing. I wish I could say the same about the expression on his face. To say he didn't look happy to see me was an understatement.

"Gia. What's up?" He fidgeted. He was wearing only his boxer shorts.

"Ty, you wouldn't believe me if I told you." I attempted to come through the door and he blocked me.

"Do you need something, Gia?"

I was embarrassed. Ty obviously had company, and I was interrupting him. I felt silly for thinking that Ty would be interested in me.

What I saw next made me feel naïve and juvenile. My mouth dropped as I watched a man with a towel wrapped around his waist leave the bedroom and head toward the bathroom. I squinted my eyes. The man's profile looked vaguely familiar.

"Terrance?" I said louder than I expected to. Terrance turned toward the door with a horrified look on his face. I looked back at Ty and looked down.

"I...um...I." I froze. I turned around and walked downstairs. I ran so quickly that I lost my footing and fell down the last four steps. A surge of pain ran over my bruised ribs.

"Gia!" Ty yelled for me as I sat there. I looked up at him, and waited for him to meet me at the bottom of the stairs. He kneeled down beside me and stroked my face.

"That bitch stood me up!" Terrance yelled from the top of the stairs.

I looked back at Ty and whispered, "Why him Ty?" I stood up, and so did Ty. He looked back up at Terrance. I walked out.

I walked for blocks and plopped down onto a park bench on the corner of Lewis and McDonough. I caught my breath and thought about Ty and Terrance.

The first time I met Ty, I thought he was smooth. He knew exactly what clothes and makeup I should wear. He sniffed my neck and picked out a perfume that suited me. All the nights we worked together at the club, I never saw him with any women.

Terrance said he called Ty repeatedly for my number. Ty ignored his calls. I thought he ignored them because he was interested in me. It was Terrance he was interested in. When he told me that first night at Ice that there was a football player in VIP checking for me, he was taken aback when I told him he could give *Terrance* my number. There were three other players with Terrance that night. It must have been another one of the players who originally told Ty that he was interested in me. But, as soon as I walked into the VIP room, Terrance was the one to talk to me and escort me out quickly.

I also remembered the conversation I had with Ty in the Chelsea Diner that made him extremely uncomfortable. I had no idea why at the time. I bragged about my ability to read people. I told Ty details about his life but left out one very important one. He was gay. He became uncomfortable thinking that, eventually, I would call him out.

And then, there was Terrance. That piece of the equation still left me baffled. He did have good fashion sense. He kept himself and his car really clean. He ordered a pomegranate martini. Those things don't make a man gay. Terrance was your typical down low brother. Nothing about him seemed gay. He even dated beautiful women, and made comments that were homophobic.

I felt disappointed – not with Terrance or Ty, but with myself. I'm ashamed to admit that the thought of losing my virginity to Ty that night crossed my mind. My inability to see something so obvious snapped me back to reality. Who was I becoming? The old Gia observed the things around her, paid close attention to detail, and tried to remove herself from all the messes that other people got themselves into. I was now part of a huge mess.

I looked down at my phone — still no call from Sam. For the first time in my life, I was really unsure of what to do. My skin crawled at the thought of the hotel I stayed at on the Grand Concourse a couple of weeks before. I looked in my wallet. After my breakfast and the new clothes I was wearing, I was down to $300.

I thought about the books I needed for the next semester. My check from the video shoot might not arrive until well after I needed it. But a roof over my head was my only priority. I could head back uptown and stay at a motel a couple of blocks from my mother's place, but there were too many people I was trying to avoid over there. I decided to go back to the Bronx.

The motel was exactly the same as it was a couple of weeks before — disgusting. People zipped in and out of the lobby. It still smelled of cigarettes and booze. I waited for the man who worked there to stop watching a talk show on the small black-and-white TV that sat on a shelf slightly below the counter I was leaning on.

"Uh mmm." I cleared my throat. He ignored me.

I opened my wallet and slammed $100 on the counter. He placed his hand over the money, slid it across the counter, picked it up, and placed it in a drawer underneath the television. He grabbed a key from the wall behind him and placed it on the counter in front of me.

"Checkout's at noon. If you return the key by then, I'll return your $50 deposit. If not, you pay for extra nights."

I took the key and walked upstairs. I dropped the two shopping bags and my purse onto the floor. I fell onto the bed and passed out.

****

It was nine AM. I'd slept for more than twelve hours. My head pounded, and my stomach growled. The last meal I ate was breakfast the day before. I walked to the bathroom and looked in the mirror. My face looked no better. I wet a washcloth and washed slowly and carefully. I'd slept in Ty's sweat suit. In rushing out of his apartment, I forgot to leave the bag for him. I skipped showering and decided to go get something to eat first.

On the way out, I gave the worker at the counter another $50. He was a different guy from the previous night.

"I'm staying another night. Room 306."

I got a bacon, egg, and cheese sandwich, orange juice, and a bottled water from the corner store down the block from the motel. I inhaled my food outside of the store in two minutes and washed it down with three big gulps of orange juice.

I walked a couple of blocks to the dollar store, which was a misnomer. Nothing I purchased was a dollar, and I ended up spending more than $20 of money I couldn't afford to spend. I picked up laundry detergent, a three-pack of underwear, socks, an oversized T-shirt to wear as pajamas, a toothbrush, and toothpaste.

I went to the laundromat and washed the T-shirt, underwear, and socks I just purchased, along with the clothes I'd bought and worn the day before. As I waited for my clothes, I took off my boots and rubbed my feet. They were killing me. I was at least thankful that I hadn't worn my open-toed shoes that night. My toes would have fallen off from frostbite by now if I had.

I checked my cell to see if I had any missed calls — still no call from Sam or anyone else. I scrolled down my incoming calls log. The last incoming call I had was from Sam the morning he met me at the diner.

I dialed Sam's cell phone number.

"For English, please press one," a recorded voice spoke back to me. I looked at the phone to make sure I'd dialed the right number. I hung up and dialed again, and again the same message. This time I pressed one.

"Please enter your wireless number and press pound," the automated voice prompted. I did as instructed and entered my telephone number.

"Thank you. Your account has been suspended. To reactivate your account, please hold for a customer care representative."

I waited.

"Hello, this is customer care. How may I assist you?"

"Yeah, my account was suspended, and I want to know why."

"Okay, and with whom am I speaking?"

"Tangia Bryant."

"Okay, well, I'm not at liberty to discuss this account with anyone but the primary account holder."

"But, I am," I paused and hung up. I was so caught up in this facade of a new life that I forgot I had nothing to my name, including the cellphone. It belonged to Ty. He must have disconnected the phone after I caught him with Terrance.

I slammed the phone on the floor, stood up, and smashed it with the heel of my boot. I sat back down, feeling defeated. I took a deep breath and rested my face in the palms of my hands. I looked up into the face of the washing machine that now spun my clothes around quickly. I felt like the clothes in the washer. I looked away, feeling dizzy. The machine stopped, and the feeling passed.

On the way to the dryer, I spotted a computer advertising Internet access near the entrance of the laundromat. I decided that if, by the time I placed my clothes in the dryer and if no one else was using it, I'd check my e-mail. As the dryer began to spin, the seat in front of the computer remained empty.

I debated as to whether I wanted to e-mail school, seeing if some special arrangement could be made to return early. Before the semester was over, I ruled out staying over the break after finding out that room and board would cost me $800.

I had an e-mail from Stephen. My hands quivered as I clicked the mouse.

Gia,

I'm starting to get worried. When we left school, I thought things were good between us. And now, I'm not sure what to think. Either you want nothing to do with me, or something bad has happened to you. I pray it's the former rather than the latter. I'm staying in New York until the 27th. Every day at noon, I'll be at the library on Fifth Avenue and 42nd. I would love for you to meet me there. If not, that's okay too. I'll see you back at school.

Stephen.

It was already the 29th. He'd left New York two days ago. Even if he was still in New York, I wasn't sure if I was ready to see him.

I deleted Stephen's e-mails and wrote to my school requesting they let me back on campus free of charge the week before the semester started.

19

NO PLACE TO CALL HOME

Two nights after I checked into the motel, I couldn't afford to stay another night. I had $50 left and needed something to get back to school with. I returned to Sam's apartment. No one was there. Police tape covered the door. There was a sign plastered there warning anyone who tried to enter that they were tampering with police evidence.

I walked to the train unsure of where to go. There was an excitement in the air that seemed to emanate from everyone except me. People walked the streets with glasses and hats that read *Happy New Year*. I walked to the entrance of Central Park on 110th. I sat on a bench tucked away behind a set of rocks beyond the ice skating rink. I placed the two bags I had under the bench. I was still wearing the thin jacket I bought at the store across the street from the diner on the east side. I crossed my arms over my chest and moved my legs, attempting to keep warm. Nothing worked. It was freezing. My nose started to drip. The wind blew. It was dry and cold, and that caused my eyes to tear up. I wiped my nose with the sleeve of my jacket and looked around.

A man slept on a bench several feet away. Unlike me,

he was bundled up. He had on a heavy coat, a sleeping bag, and several blankets. Unlike me, he had more than two bags. He had about ten. I thought about the homeless woman on the train I saw my first night back in the city. The train was warm, and that's where I decided to go.

I headed to the train and ducked when a pigeon flew at my face. The train was sounding better by the minute.

I started off on the 3 train and rode it into Times Square. I switched to the Q train and rode it all the way into Queens. I rode the Q train back into Times Square and took the A to the last stop in Far Rockaway. I got back on the A and rode it all the way to Washington Heights. I took the A train back to Harlem and transferred to the D. I dozed off somewhere between 125th and Brighton Beach.

I was groggy when I saw my mother in a fog, kneeling next to me on the subway platform. It was sixteen years ago and she smoothed out my hair and wiped the corners of my mouth with her fingers. Every muscle in her body moved at once and I saw the desperation in her eyes. She glanced at the train approaching the station.

"Okay, Gia." She handed me a cup that held a couple of pennies. I staggered forward like the toddler I was. "It's show time, baby girl. Now show momma what you're gonna do."

I shook the cup and repeated the lines she taught me earlier that night.

"Please help us," I said to the grown-ups walking by. "My momma and I are just trying to get enough change together to get something to eat. Any change you can give will be a big help. Thank you."

"Louder, Gia! Louder! I can barely hear you!"

"But, mommy. I'm tired." The train stopped, and the doors opened. She held my hand and put on a pair of sunglasses. She hung her head, and I led her into the train, pretending I was leading my blind mother inside. There was no need to change the expression on my face. There was no need to fake being tired or desolate. I shook the cup and repeated my lines until my mother had collected enough money for her hit for the night.

An MTA employee woke me up and my mother was gone.

"Excuse me, ma'am. This is the last stop on this train."

"Where am I?" I looked down at my hand for my mother's cup of change.

"You're at the Coney Island station. Last stop on this train. You need to get off."

"Oh." I straightened up and looked around the empty train. "Wow, I'm so exhausted. I missed my stop." I picked up my bags and walked across the platform to take the D train in the opposite direction.

I rode the trains the entire night. Because I was well dressed and clean, I didn't think anyone would suspect I was homeless. People came in and out of the trains drunk and screaming, "Happy New Year," all night long. I rode a total of seven trains that night through four different boroughs. I re-emerged at nine AM squinting and jumpy. I used my remaining dollars to buy an Egg McMuffin at the McDonald's on 42nd Street.

There was a lot less confetti and trash on the street than I expected. Clean-up crews must have started the moment the ball dropped. There were very few people on the street. I assumed most of them passed out a couple hours before after a night of partying and ringing in the New Year.

I ate slowly though I was starving. I sipped a cup of coffee to help me stay awake though I hated the taste. I left my trash on the table well after I finished eating so the staff would know I was a paying customer and wouldn't rush me out. I closed my eyes for what I anticipated being a minute.

I jumped when someone touched my shoulder. It was one of McDonald's employees.

"I'm sorry, miss, but you can't sleep here."

"I'm sorry." I smoothed out my clothes and hair. "Wild night of partying. I need to go home and get to bed."

"Lucky. I was stuck here working all night," he said.

I faked a laugh and looked away.

"Can I take your tray for you?"

"Um," I hesitated. "Yeah, I'm done."

He carried my tray away as I stood up. It was almost eleven AM. I walked down 42nd Street toward the east side. I turned down Fifth Avenue and sat on the stairs of the New York Public Library.

Not knowing what else to do on the steps of the closed library, I recited a poem by Langston Hughes[4] that I memorized during the semester.

Kid in the Park
Lonely little question mark
On a bench in the park:
See the people passing by?
See the airplanes in the sky?
See the birds
Flying home
Before dark?
Home's just around
The corner there –
But not really
Anywhere

My eyes started to tear from the cold. Eventually, those tears mixed with ones full of anger, depression, and pain — tears that attempted to cleanse me of everything I had been through. I thought of the last two weeks and the last eighteen years. Tears dripped and my nose drained down the stairs of the library. My tears were making up for all the times I suffocated them in my throat. My body refused to hold the pent-up emotion any longer. I was short of breath and started to hyperventilate; the way a baby does when she's cried too much.

I felt a hand on my shoulder. I didn't look up, thinking that whoever was standing behind me would tell me I couldn't sit there. I wasn't ready to move.

The hand placed a tissue in my lap. I wiped my face and looked up.

It was Stephen. He sat down on the stairs next to me.

"Gia. Your face. What happened to you?" he asked, referring to the bruises and my tears.

"Stephen? I thought you were leaving on the 27th."

"Hey Stephen. Everything okay over here?"

I looked up at a woman standing over us. She wore the same Long Island Christian Church baseball cap as Stephen.

"No. I'm okay," he responded. "I'm going to be here for a while. You and the others can go. I'll be okay."

"Okay." The woman walked away and joined the rest of their group.

"I was planning on leaving," he continued. "I was really enjoying the work with the church, so I decided to stay a little longer. I was also hoping I'd see you." He placed his hand on my thigh.

An awkward laughter escaped through my tears.

"Where have you been?" he asked.

"Stephen," I looked into his eyes. "I'm freezing and tired." I started to sob. He put his arm around me. I put my face into his chest and soaked his shirt with my tears. He asked questions once I stopped.

"Where are you staying? I kept trying to call your mother's house. The phone's disconnected. I went to the Center again, and Gladys said she hasn't seen you since I did."

"It's a really long story, Stephen." I knew I'd have to explain soon.

"Well, I was heading back to my parent's house in Boston today, but I had to come check one last time to see if you'd meet me here. And here you are." He looked into my eyes, smiling in disbelief.

"Where are you staying?" I sniffled.

"In Long Island with my aunt and uncle. Gia, we need to get you out of this cold. Do you want to go get something to eat?"

"I already ate."

"Well, is it cool if we spend some time together before I go back to Boston?"

"Stephen, I'm homeless. I have nowhere *to* spend time with you," I blurted out. The tears resumed.

"What?" he asked, taken aback. "Where have you been staying?" He seemed angry. I looked toward the train station and he followed my glance.

"Gia," he whispered sympathetically, "you slept on the train?"

"Well, I didn't sleep much. I rode the train the entire night. The night before that I was in a motel in the Bronx, but I ran out of money."

"Why didn't you call me?"

I looked down unable to answer his question. I crossed my arms and rubbed them.

"Come on, Gia. I'm parked in a garage around the block.

"Where are we going?"

"To warm you up."

We drove a couple blocks to 47th and Lexington. Stephen pulled his car into the garage next to the Radisson Hotel. I looked at him suspiciously.

"Look, Stephen. I don't think you know who you're dealing with. I might be down, but I'm not out."

"I'll go back to my aunt and uncle's place in Long Island.

You can stay here as long as you need. Call me when you're ready to talk."

I immediately felt bad for assuming he was trying to take advantage of me.

"Stephen, I'm sorry."

"Don't be, Gia. You've had a really rough night. I understand." I rubbed my eyes. Although the car ride to the hotel was all of five minutes, I had a hard time keeping my eyes open.

"Come on. Let's get you a room."

The hotel was much different from the one on the Grand Concourse. The doorman was not dressed in clothes saturated in dirt. He didn't smell like the bar down the street and he didn't beg for my money. He wore a suit the shade of midnight and greeted me when I walked in. Stephen followed behind me, carrying my two plastic shopping bags.

The lobby smelled antiseptic and piney. Instead of carpet, the floor was tiled. The employees behind the front desk assisted customers, and from what I could tell, the monitors they were looking at behind the counter were computers and not televisions.

Stephen stepped up to the counter.

"Hi. I need a room please."

"Okay." The attendant smiled and punched something into the keyboard.

"How many nights will you be staying sir?"

"Five, please."

"Five?" I asked.

"Or longer if you need it." He shifted his attention to me. I shifted my body weight from one leg to the other and started to do the calculations in my head. If this hotel was $150 a night, and I was pretty sure it was more than that, and I was spending at least four nights there if not more, Stephen would be spending $600 for me to have a place to stay. I normally would have protested, but my fatigue and lack of options prevented me.

"Okay. We have a room available. Can I have a credit card for incidentals, please? And if you'd like, we can charge your stay on this card upon checkout."

"That's fine." He nodded and smiled.

"Will you be needing two keys?" He looked at me.

"Gia, you want an extra key, or is one enough?"

"I'll take two." The woman prepared the keys and handed them to Stephen. "You're in room 1050. Enjoy your stay."

"Thanks." He faced me and handed me the keys. "Okay, Gia. I'm going to head out to Long Island. Call me when you're ready. Can I have a pen and a piece of paper?" he asked the woman behind the counter.

"Certainly." She handed him a pen and a pad and he scribbled down his cell number. "Use the phone in the room to call me. Don't worry about the bill."

"Stephen. I–"

"You don't need to thank me. Go upstairs and get some rest. Just call me when you can."

"Okay, Stephen." I hesitated, stepped forward, and hugged him.

He squeezed me tight and whispered into my ear, "I'm glad you're safe, Gia."

I let go. He smiled and handed me my bags. We waited until I got in the elevator and waved goodbye as the doors closed.

The room had the same smell as the lobby and was as clean as the doorman. The king-sized bed against the wall called out to me as I put my bags down.

I went into the bathroom to get a towel to place over the pillow. Fatigue battled with my desire to take a shower in a clean tub, something I hadn't done in several days.

I turned down the bed and realized I didn't need the towel. The sheets were ivory white and I couldn't resist them. I changed into Ty's sweats and crawled under the blankets.

I turned on the TV. There was a *Twilight Zone* marathon on channel 11. It was one of my favorite shows, and I hated my eyes for not staying open long enough to watch more than half an episode. I'd seen it every New Year's Day for the last five years. The episode was called *Five Characters Looking for an Exit*. In the episode, an army officer, a clown, a ballerina, a bagpiper, and a hobo are all stuck in a room with no exit. Unsure of where they are or how they got there, they try everything to escape the confines of the four walls. Finally, after the five characters successfully form a human tower, the army officer is able to escape. His victory is short-lived when he is thrown back into the room, which is actually a toy box filled with the five characters, all of whom are toy dolls, unable to escape their dwelling.

I slept through the night and into the next afternoon, almost a full twenty-four hours. I stumbled into the shower and stayed there for an hour. The water stayed hot the entire time.

After my shower, I reentered the *Twilight Zone*, and considered calling Stephen during commercial breaks. Eight commercial breaks later, I did.

"Hello?" he answered on the first ring.

"Hey, Stephen. It's Gia."

"Hey, Gia. How did you sleep?"

"I just woke up a couple of hours ago." I twisted the telephone cord around my finger.

"Good. Did you eat something?"

"No. I was hoping you'd meet me for an early dinner?"

"What are you in the mood for?" His voice perked up.

"I don't know. Do you like West Indian food?"

"I love it."

"Okay, so when can you be here? Because my stomach is

talking to me right now."

He laughed. "I'll be there in an hour. And while you're waiting, have something from the minibar. It'll automatically get charged to the room."

"I don't drink, Stephen."

"I know. There are sodas and snacks in there too. Help yourself." I felt embarrassed by my ignorance.

"Okay."

"So, I'll see you in an hour."

I met Stephen in the lobby an hour later. He stood up from one of the oversized plush chairs that decorated the lobby. I laughed thinking that, if he'd sat in the chair any longer, it might swallow him.

Stephen looked great as usual. I wished I could say the same about myself. I looked down at the clothes I was wearing for the third day in a row. I ironed them out with the palms of my hands, as if that would somehow make them new.

"Hey, Gia." Stephen hugged me. I still had to get used to this hugging thing. I wasn't ready to wrap my arms around him. They were more comfortable in a semicircle, loosely around his waist, my hands giving him a couple of pats between his shoulder blades.

"So, where we going?" His smile consumed his face.

"To the village. But do you mind if we take a ride uptown really quick?" I asked.

"I don't mind at all. Do you mind? Your stomach won't yell at me, will it?"

"No." I smiled. "I had a $5 bag of M&Ms from the minibar, so I'll be good for a little while."

"Money well spent." He pulled out of the garage next to the hotel. "So, where we headed?"

"East 117th Street. Hop on the FDR, and take it to 125th Street."

"Okay." He didn't ask any questions. I decided to explain the situation anyway.

"A lot's gone on over the past couple of weeks, Stephen."

He nodded quietly.

"We'll talk over dinner."

"Whenever you're ready."

We arrived at Sam's place fifteen minutes later. "You can double-park here." I pointed to a spot in front of the building. I shouldn't be long."

"Take your time."

"If the cops come, just circle the block and come park back in this spot, so you don't get a ticket."

"Will do."

The police tape was gone. I banged on the door as if I could open it with the force of my fist.

There was no answer. I knocked again.

"Who?" A voice that sounded like it hadn't slept in days asked.

"It's Gia," I screamed through the door. The chains chimed as the door was unlocked. Sam looked almost as bad as I did after I got jumped.

He stepped out of the apartment and hugged me. He squeezed me so tight that I thought he would leave fingerprints in my back.

"Come in." He finally let go and escorted me inside. "Sit down, G."

I looked around the apartment. It looked like my mother's. There were things thrown everywhere, like someone had picked it up and shaken it. Sam must have known what I was thinking.

"You'd think they'd clean up after themselves. They tore this place up looking for Dee's drugs." He shook his head. "I can't believe she played me like that. And then she had the nerve to try to pull my name into it to get a lighter sentence.

But I was cleared of everything. Working a twelve-hour day is a hell of an alibi. Where you been, Gia? I tried calling your cell."

"I was in the Bronx. I just got back into Manhattan yesterday."

"I didn't get back home until this morning. The holiday had me in jail longer than I needed to be."

"My cell's not on anymore. Are my things still here?"

"Yeah, they're in the room. They went through your things too, Gia. I would have picked them up for you if I was back sooner. I'm sorry."

"It's okay. I can get them together." I stood up and walked into my room. My things were thrown everywhere. I threw a pair of jeans and a sweater on the bed. I shoved the rest of my clothes into my bag. Underneath one of the many piles was my jewelry box. One of the arms had been amputated from a combination of rust and the fall it probably took from my bag to the floor. I wrapped it in one of my dresses and placed it in my bag.

Once all my things were packed, I took the clothes I placed on the bed and changed into them. I made the bed and tried to make the room look as nice as it did when Sam gave it to me. I heard a knock on the door and turned around.

"Come in."

"Wow," Sam said, looking around. "That was quick."

"Yeah. I'll come by in a couple of days to help you clean up the rest of the place."

"Nah, G. You don't need to do that. Let me help you with your bags." He picked them up and walked out to the car with me. Stephen popped the trunk when he saw us and got out to help.

"Stephen, this is Sam. Sam, Stephen."

"Hey. Good to meet you, Sam." Stephen shook Sam's hand. "I'll take that," Stephen said, reaching for my bag.

"Sam's like a brother to me. I've been staying with him the last couple of weeks."

Stephen placed my bags in the trunk and slammed it closed.

"Gia's my little sister. You hurt her and you answer to me," he said, roughly patting Stephen on the back.

"I'll take good care of her," Stephen said and looked at me.

"Can you give me and Gia a minute, Stephen?"

"Yeah, no problem. I'll be in the car."

Sam pulled out an envelope from his pocket and placed it in my hand.

"Here, Gia. Please take this back. I meant it when I said you're like a little sister to me. I also know how broke college students are."

We both laughed.

"Sam, are you sure?" I didn't want to take the money back, but I could really use it.

"Positive."

"Thanks." I put the envelope into my pocketbook. I gave Sam a hug — a real one. I was overwhelmed by how much this man looked out for me. We truly were family.

"I'll see you soon, Sam."

"Gia, you know you're more than welcome to stay here with me."

"Thanks for the offer, Sam. But I'm going back to school sooner than I anticipated."

"Don't forget about the little people when you make it to the top. You have an amazing future ahead of you."

"Thanks, Sam."

"All right." He walked me to the passenger side of Stephen's car. "See you soon." I waved goodbye to Sam as Stephen drove off.

"Now, I just have to warn you, Stephen. For real West

Indian food, I'd need to take you into a hole in the wall in Crown Heights. But the place we're going has a really cool vibe, and the food is decent."

I smiled at the thought of a nice dinner. I had never been to this restaurant but heard great things. The smell of curry and jerk greeted us before the hostess did when we arrived. I inhaled deeply, accepting their salutations.

"How many?" the hostess asked.

"Two, please."

She grabbed two menus from her podium. "Follow me, please."

We followed her upstairs to a balcony that overlooked the main level, where people ate and a jazz band played the classic, *Take Five*. Palm trees shaded the band from the flickering votive centerpieces, making the dining room come to life.

"Nice pick, Gia." Stephen gawked at the décor and smiled.

"Thanks." I opened my menu.

"You recommend something?"

"Stephen," I said, putting down the menu. "If I don't get this all off my chest now, I probably never will."

He put down his menu and looked into my eyes.

"Hold on a second." He lifted his hand, motioning for the waitress. "Excuse me. Can we have two glasses of water, and I'll call you over when we're ready to order our food. Is that okay?"

"Of course it is." She smiled.

"Okay. Sorry about that, Gia. I just wanted to make sure we don't have a bunch of interruptions."

I nodded my head and continued. "I really wasn't looking forward to coming back home when the semester ended. I would have stayed on campus if it weren't for the $800 they were going to charge me. My first night back, I spent at my mother's house. I left the next day because she stole my money."

The busboy brought the water over at the perfect time. I

swallowed hard as if the water would remove the bad taste that the words were leaving in my mouth. It didn't, but I continued anyway.

"My mother's addicted to crack. She has been since I was a baby and before that even. The first day I was home from school, she stole my money to buy drugs." I searched his face for disgust but I couldn't find it. He didn't flinch and I continued.

"Because she stole my money, I packed my things and went to look for my brother, who I found out got arrested and is in jail. He put me in contact with a friend of his – Sam – the guy you just met. I stayed with him until his girl got busted for selling drugs out of his apartment. After the police investigation and the fear of getting arrested myself, I was forced to leave Sam's place, so I stayed in a motel in the Bronx. After my money ran out, I rode the train all night."

I finished off the rest of my water. He took a sip of his water and leaned in closer.

"Why were you so ashamed to tell me that, Gia? None of the things that happened to you were in your control. None of those things were a result of anything you did wrong."

I took my napkin and wiped the sides of mouth.

"When we met, I knew right away there was no way that you could possibly relate to the life I left behind in New York, and honestly, that's part of the reason I liked you so much. You knew nothing about my crazy childhood or my crazy life back at home, and you liked me. I was afraid–"

"Gia." He reached across the table to grab my hand. "You are *the* most beautiful, intriguing, and intelligent woman I have ever met. All families have their issues, and everyone has their problems. True, we grew up in very different families under very different circumstances, but none of that matters to me. Since the second we left school, not a second goes by without the thought of you passing through my mind.

It doesn't make any sense. Not knowing where you were or how to get in contact with you was the worst feeling I've had in a long time. I'm not going to pretend that I can understand all that you've been through. What I do know is that, from this point on, I want to be a part of your life, and I want you to be a part of mine. I'm in love with you, Gia."

I was speechless. I did have feelings for Stephen, but wasn't sure if I was in love with him. And if I was unsure, it probably meant that I wasn't.

"Stephen, since I was very little, not only have I been handed the short end of the stick, but I've been beaten with it — over and over again. I learned from a very young age to protect myself. In doing that, I've built up a wall so high that I'm not even sure if *I* can tear it down. And to be honest, I don't know if I'll ever really want to. I'm not sure how you fit into all of this, Stephen. I went away to college knowing it was my only way out of the situation I came from. I don't play a sport, I don't sing, and I don't act. I want to rise above what I came from and move on. School is the only way I can do that. So, I've tried everything to keep those two parts of my life very separate from each other."

"That's all good and well, but part of the beauty of who we are is the challenges that we've overcome throughout life. I'm not saying you gotta tell everyone and their momma every scary detail of your life. But there will be people who are genuinely interested in you and want to get to know you — all of you." He squeezed my hand.

I fidgeted and he withdrew.

"Sorry, Stephen. I hear what you're saying, and maybe that works for you, but it doesn't work all that well for me. Trust me."

I thought about the last couple of weeks and how I let my wall down and let a couple of people in. Dee, Ty, and Terrance all disappointed me. Now, Stephen was echoing Ty's words. *Did you ever think someone might genuinely want to get to know you, Gia?*

I still wasn't convinced.

We sat silently until my stomach spoke loud and clear. I cleared my throat and shifted in my seat. Stephen laughed and motioned for the waitress.

"So, Gia," he said later as I took the last couple of bites of my jerk chicken. "My aunt and uncle would really love to have you over for lunch tomorrow."

"Um," I looked down at my plate and made my macaroni and cheese dance around with my fork.

"It's just lunch, Gia. It's not even dinner. Nothing fancy."

I sighed and thought it was the least I could do. But I was uncomfortable with the idea.

"Stephen, I'm sure they're really great people, but I'm honestly not even close to ready for all that."

"I understand."

"Thanks. You ready to get out of here?"

"Yeah, let's go." He paid the bill and drove me back to the hotel.

20

THE CITY THROUGH A NEW SET OF EYES

Once again, I overslept. I didn't sweat it, figuring it wasn't oversleeping if I had nowhere to go. I probably could have slept through the day if the phone hadn't rung at noon.

"Hello?" I answered.

"Gia, it's lunch time!" Stephen's voice was annoyingly perky. I looked at the alarm clock on the nightstand in disbelief. But he was right, it was noon.

"Yeah, I guess you're right, which means I slept through breakfast."

"I'm sorry. Did I wake you?"

"No, it's okay. It was time to wake up anyway."

"Okay. You want to grab lunch?"

"Okay. Are you in Long Island?"

"Yeah. Is two good?"

"Yeah, that's perfect."

"Okay. And if you don't have any plans for the evening, there's somewhere I want to take you."

"Where?"

"You'll see. I guarantee you'll love it."

"Well, I'd really love it if you'd tell me where it was."

"You'll just have to wait and see." He laughed.

"Okay, Stephen. I'll see you in a couple of hours."

After a late lunch at V's Real BBQ in Times Square, we strolled up Broadway. Stephen walked slowly like a typical tourist. It was his second time visiting New York and his first time visiting as an adult. I envied the way he talked about the city as we walked through Times Square. To him, every building was beautiful. The crowds were exciting. I wish I could see the city the way he did. Instead it disgusted me. I felt like a woman trapped inside an abusive relationship. No matter how much the city beat me down, there was no escaping it.

We stopped in front of an unusual building on 51st Street. It looked like the entrance to a theater, but something was different about it. I read the sign on the awning.

"Is this a church or a theater?"

"It's both." He smiled. If he told me we were going to listen to poetry in a church, I probably wouldn't have agreed to go. But now that I was there, there was no turning back. I looked down at the clothes I was wearing. I looked at Stephen. Neither of us was dressed for church. By the looks of it, neither was anyone else going in.

The church was an old Broadway theater. When we entered the sanctuary, my heart beat in an unfamiliar erratic rhythm and my throat tightened. It looked nothing like my grandmother's old church, but there she was, sitting in the front row and motioning me to come over. Suddenly, I was five again and we were the only people in the world.

She patted the seat next to her and I sat in it. She straightened out my dress, making sure it wasn't tucked into my tights after my trip to the bathroom.

"Amen," she said. I was always amazed by my grandmother's ability to listen to the sermon, straighten out my hair and dress, and respond to the preacher's prompts.

The pastor read something out of the Bible in old English that was next to impossible for a five-year-old to understand. My grandmother leaned her head down toward my ear and explained,

"Joseph was sold into slavery by his brothers, but God gave him the special gift of interpreting people's dreams. He interpreted the dreams of the king of Egypt, and because of this, the king gave him a very important position in the land of Egypt. When Joseph's brothers were in trouble, they came to him for help. And, even though they'd disowned him, he forgave them and helped them when they were in need," she explained.

I nodded and couldn't take my eyes off of her. My grandmother was the prettiest and smartest woman in the world.

"Gia, is here okay?"

"Huh?" I asked, slowly snapping out my daydream.

"These seats. Are they okay?" He pointed to two seats about ten rows from the front.

If it was a Broadway show we came to see, I'd have been excited to sit so close to the front. The last time I was in church, I was six years old. It was for my grandmother's funeral. I was angry that God took away the only person I loved. I decided then that I would never go back to church. I felt angry with Stephen for tricking me into coming. On the other hand, I felt it was the least I could do in return for what he was doing for me. I looked toward the back of the church, wishing I could sit there and blend into the background. I couldn't. The seats in the back were roped off. I wondered why. Maybe they were reserved for the worst sinners – the ones who, if they even showed up to church in first place, would inevitably be late. Could I explain to the usher that I was one of those bad people but just always made a point of being on time, and maybe I could sit in one of those comfortable seats in the back?

I sighed, knowing I was being ridiculous and this was a losing battle. I followed Stephen into the row near the front and took my seat.

I quickly stood back up as the people around me did. They got their cue from the rising stage curtain that looked as thick and heavy as red velvet cake. About a dozen people who looked to be around my age, stood with microphones in their hands on two risers on the stage. A black woman who looked to be in her thirties began to sing.

Come lay down the burdens you have carried, for in the sanctuary, God is here. He is here! He is here! To break the yoke and lift the heavy burden. He is here! He is here! To mend your heart and come and bless the broken. So come cast down the burdens you have carried, for in the sanctuary, God is here.

The sounds that came from her mouth were so sweet; I could practically taste them. I thought she accidently stepped into the wrong building. She should have been on the stage across the street, starring in the Tony Award-winning musical that was playing there. But instead, she was here, singing about God.

I looked around, seeing if her words were true, looking for a God I wasn't convinced existed. Instead, I saw a crowd of a hundred young people. Some had their eyes closed, some had their hands raised, and others just sat motionless. I turned back around, drawn to the beauty of the woman's voice. She spoke when the song ended. Her background singers exited, and the crowd sat back down.

"Good evening, everyone. Tonight, we have an amazing night of poetry, music and testimonies for you. We welcome you to our church home and hope that you enjoy the evening. Please know that the poetry, music, and testimonies shared tonight come from very real and true places. Music is a gift from God, the poetry a reflection of God's intelligence and creativity, and the testimonies a witness of how God moves in the lives of ordinary individuals like you and me. So, sit back, relax, and enjoy the evening. Thank you."

She exited the stage and was replaced by a man who looked to be in his early thirties. His opening words caught my attention.

"My father was addicted to drugs, my mother was addicted to drugs, and as a newborn baby, so was I. I was a crack baby. That's the label they gave me. I practically raised myself. At the age of eleven, I started robbing, stealing, and selling drugs. By age thirteen, I was in and out of detention centers and foster homes. When I was eighteen, I got locked up for ten years. Some of the best years of my life were spent in confinement. When I was in prison, one of the older men there who was serving a life sentence shared a Bible verse with me. It said, 'I will restore to you the years the locust have stolen.' If you don't know anything about locusts, all you need to know is this. They destroy everything in sight, all vegetation that is meant to be beautiful, all vegetation that is meant to produce fruits and vegetables and foods that sustain us. Sometimes, the locusts eat so much that there seems to be nothing left. But in that verse, God promises to restore all that. After hearing that verse for the first time, I wondered if God could restore not only the years I spent in jail, but the years of my childhood that were stolen because of the drug addiction and messed-up situation I was born into. So I prayed — nothing fancy, just straight-up real talk with God. And, those prayers were answered. God allowed me to get out of jail before I turned thirty. He restored all of those years. I was able to go to college and get a job, despite having a record. I have a wife and a beautiful family that I am able to love despite the lack of love I received growing up."

His eyes filled with tears, and he bit his bottom lip. He clenched his fist and pointed to the sky, while he continued speaking. "It was all because of God that those things happened. And, you are no different from me. No matter what it is that the locusts have stolen from you, God wants to restore it, only if you'll allow him." He wiped the tears from his eyes and exited the stage.

The crowd rose and applauded. The metaphor of the locusts and his imagery caused me to miss my love for good literature. I read poetry since returning to the city, but I didn't read half as much as I did during the semester. Like the locusts, I devoured the pages of books as if my life depended on it. Not only did I read my assigned readings for class, but I read because I loved to. I wondered if the Bible was full of the same beautiful imagery he just spoke about.

Next, a young woman came on stage and read a poem.

If you knit me together in my mother's womb,
Why do I feel so unraveled?
And if you said you'd never leave me or forsake me,
Why do I feel so alone?
And if you say in you I live, move, and have my being,
Why do I feel so stagnant?
And if you promised that in your strength anything is possible
Why do I feel so incompetent?
But then I remember you, hanging on that cross.
Limbs stretched out being pulled in all different directions
The way I feel now
And you even whispered to God thinking that He'd forsaken you
The way I think now.
And you too felt weak
The way I do now.
You died, but resurrected to sit in a beautiful paradise.

At the right hand of the Father.
My spirit as dead as your flesh once was
You resurrect me to a beautiful paradise.
Forever under the refuge of your wings.
Forever a daughter of the King of Kings.

She continued once the applause died down.

"I wrote this poem because there are times when God doesn't seem to exist. It seems like He lets bad things happen to us and that He's left us all alone to fend for ourselves. He didn't promise that things would be easy, but He did promise that, in Him, we'll always find refuge. So if there's something that's causing you a lot of pain and hurt, know that God cares about you. He loves you and is just waiting for you to love Him back."

The crowd clapped again. My throat grew tight, and my eyes were wet. I remembered hearing about finding refuge under God's wings but couldn't remember when or from whom I'd heard it. I felt uneasy about what was going on. I fought back tears and hung my head.

"You okay, Gia?" Stephen leaned toward me with concern.

"Yeah, I'm fine." I looked back at the stage.

The rest of the night was more of the same. I continued to be intrigued by the poetry, prose, imagery, and symbolism from the Bible. I later learned that many of the songs that were sung and poems that were read were based on Bible verses.

There was an altar call at the end of the service. People were invited to go to the altar to pray if they felt like what they heard touched them. What I heard that night had some sort of impact on me, but I needed time to figure out what that impact was. I decided I didn't need to go to the altar to figure it out. I'd do it on my own.

"Are you ready to go, Gia?"

"Yeah." I got up.

The gaudy lights of Times Square shocked my senses and reminded me of the vivid imagery I'd just heard.

"Hey, Stephen. Can I ask you something?"

"Of course. Ask me anything." He smiled and looked into my eyes.

"You read the Bible?"

"Yeah, I do."

I clenched my teeth and swallowed. "How, or where–"

He interrupted me. "I have an extra one if you want to read it. Are you interested in it?"

"Yeah. I'm not saying I believe what's in it or anything. I just think from a literary perspective..."

"You don't have to explain it to me. I'll get you one as soon as we get back to school."

"Cool." I paused. "Thanks, Stephen. I really enjoyed my-self tonight."

"You're welcome, Gia." He grabbed my hand. We walked to the hotel hand in hand, and this time I didn't let go. We stopped at the entrance.

"I won't be able to see you tomorrow, Stephen. I need to go see Micah."

"Okay, no problem. Do what you have to do, and I'll see you the day after tomorrow. Is that's cool?"

"Okay. Oh, and Stephen, thanks again. I never imagined church could actually be enjoyable."

"Yeah. Can't knock it till you try it."

"You're right. Well, good night." We hugged and waved one last goodbye as I walked up the front steps to the lobby.

"Hey, Gia, by the way. If you can't wait to get back to school, most hotels have Bibles right in the room you can read. Check the nightstand."

"Okay." I smiled. "Good night."

"Night, Gia."

21

SILVER LININGS

Micah seemed a lot better than he did the last time I saw him. He was clean and he'd cut his braids off. I smiled in admiration of his new cut.

He hugged me and lifted me off the ground.

"Baby sis! Where you been?" His smile faded when he got a closer look at my face.

"Yo, Gia. What the hell happened to your face?" I touched it self-consciously. Janay and her friends messed me up so much that it still looked puffy and uneven, even after it began to heal. I didn't want to worry Micah, so I lied.

"I took a really bad fall in Sam's building. I was in a rush and slipped on some ice on the stairs. Nothing's broken. I'm fine." His eyes narrowed as if he were trying to read the bruises on my face.

"I know you're lying, G." He was obviously angry. I changed the subject.

"Sorry it's been a while since I've seen you. Things have been crazy."

"Gia, you wouldn't lie to me, right?" Lines formed on his forehead and around his chin.

"Everything is fine. Just trying to get everything ready for going back to school." I figured I'd spare the truth and details until a later time. Micah was so stressed the last time I saw him that I didn't want to see him like that again.

Some of the tension released from his face. "Aight, G. How's my dude, Sam?"

"Sam's good. As soon as he stops working for a second, he'll come out and see you. He needs a serious vacation." Again, I spared the details of the situation with Sam. If Micah knew I wasn't staying there anymore, he'd worry. "So, how you feel, Micah? I was worried about you the last time I was here."

"Yeah, Gia. This place can get you down. I can't imagine being up in here for the next ten years. I'm a young man. I'll miss out on some of the best years of my life. But, I have to man up, live with the consequences of my actions. Know what I mean, sis?"

Although the thought of Micah being in jail for ten years made me sick, I smiled at his maturation.

"There was something else that was bothering me last time you stopped by." His expression darkened and his eyes appeared wet. He paused. "You're going to be an auntie, Gia."

"What!" My jaw dropped. The smile on Micah's face was contagious, and I caught it. "Congrats, Mich."

"Yeah, thanks. The last time you were here, I was really depressed at the thought of my kid being damn near ten years old by the time I got up out of here. I hated thinking of her coming up in here at such a young age to visit. What kind of example would I be? But then, I thought I could still be a good dad and that she could learn from my mistake, you know? I want her to have a better life than I did. It also doesn't hurt that she'll have a college-educated auntie to look up to."

"She?"

"Yeah, G. I'm having a girl." A tear fell from his left eye. He lowered his head and wiped the tear away.

"Micah, don't worry about the time that you'll spend in here. Just be the best dad you can." I paused. "And, Micah, I think God will restore the time you've lost in this place."

"God?" There was tension in his forehead, and the lines returned. "I think that's the first time I ever heard you talk about God."

After the words came out of my mouth, I looked around the room to see where they came from. I'm not sure why I said it, but I remembered the man the night before who spoke of being in prison, coming out, and having a beautiful wife and family. I thought it might encourage Micah.

"Do you believe in God, Mich?" I asked, anxiously awaiting Micah's answer.

"Yeah, I believe in God. I might not be perfect and I've done some messed up things in my life, but I pray every day that He'll get me out of this place." I nodded, hoping that God would answer his prayer.

"Aight, so you ready to do this?" He pulled a piece of paper out of his back pocket.

"I'm ready."

Micah looked at the paper. "*Caged Bird* by Maya Angelou[5]. A free bird leps."

"*Leaps*," I corrected him.

"Leaps," he continued. "On the back of the wind and floats downst...downst-re...downstream–"

"Good, Micah," I encouraged him. "Keep going."

"Till the cur-rent ends, and dips his wings in the or... oran...orange sun rays and dars–"

"*Dares.*"

"Dares to clam...no, claim...the sky."

"Micah, you did great. Want me to finish?" He nodded

and shoved the scrap of paper across the table. I looked at him like a proud parent. He closed his eyes and listened to me finish the poem.

But a bird that stalks down his narrow cage
Can seldom see through his bars of rage
His wings are clipped and his feet are tied
So he opens his throat to sing.
The caged bird sings
With a fearful trill
Of things unknown
But longed for still
And his tune is heard
On the distant hill
For the caged bird sings of freedom.

I looked up. Micah's eyes were closed and tears streamed down his cheeks. His smile peeked through the tears.

****

I headed downtown to see if Cliff was at his office. I pulled out Cliff's card, forgetting his office suite number.

"Hi, I need to go the twelfth floor," I said to the guard sitting behind the desk.

"Who are you here to see, please?" He pushed a clipboard toward me.

"Clifford Harrison."

"Sign in, please." I signed my name. He handed me a badge and pressed a button that allowed me through a turn style.

I walked into the lobby of Cliff's office.

"Gia." Cliff called me from the doorway of his office down the hall.

"Hey, Cliff. I'm here to sign the paperwork."

"Sit down, Gia. Your face looks better." He looked up at me briefly. He grabbed some papers from his file cabinet, pushed them toward me, and examined my face.

"Where do I sign?" I lifted the clipboard, attempting to draw his attention away from my face.

"Sign and date the bottom, and fill out all the information at the top of the page, including your social. Listen, Gia. Sorry about the other day. Business is business and they–"

"Cliff," I said, interrupting him. "You don't need to explain. I get it. If I still get paid for the day I worked, I don't really care."

"The check will be mailed to you in about two weeks." I kept writing and he kept speaking. "By the way, you might be interested to know that you're still in the video."

"I am?" I looked at him with shock.

"Yeah. The director decided that the footage you shot on the day you worked was really good and was all he needed to tell the story. Apparently, you and Jah's chemistry was so good off camera that they are using some still pictures they took while they weren't shooting, to add to the video."

"Hmm," I said, thinking of the way Jahzelle blew me off when he saw my jacked-up face.

"So, you headed back to school soon?" Cliff asked.

"Yeah, sooner than later, I hope."

"Good for you. Finish your education. I have to say, I was impressed when you walked on set with your face looking like it did. That took some serious guts."

I laughed. "Yeah, it did look pretty bad, didn't it?"

Cliff nodded and laughed.

"Give me a call when you graduate. You have perseverance and some serious negotiation skills that this office could really use."

I was flattered that Cliff was offering me a job on the business end of things rather than in front of the camera. It was much more of a challenge for me to use my brain to get paid then it was to use my body. I took another one of his cards, just in case.

"I'm going to hold you to that offer, Cliff. But I demand to have Saturdays off." I smiled.

"I told you I work every day of the week. But, you're right. I do need to get out of this office."

I looked at his card and put it in my wallet.

"Thanks, Cliff."

"Aight, Gia. Take care of yourself."

When I got back to the hotel, I checked my e-mail at the hotel's business center. There was an e-mail from my school.

Dear Gia,

Upon review of your request, we are allowing you to return to school on Monday, January 10th, under the condition that you participate in a work study program to help offset your room and board fees.

If you have any questions, please contact Residence Life at 401-555-7723.

Sincerely,

Brown University Department of Student Life.

I logged out and got up. I walked back to my room and dropped everything to call Stephen.

"Hello?"

"Stephen? It's Gia."

"Are you okay, Gia. What's wrong?" I was breathing heavily, regretting being too impatient to wait on the elevator.

"I'm going back to school in two days."

"What? That's amazing! Tell me about it."

"Well, I sent an e-mail to Residence Life requesting to return early. I explained my financial situation, and they're letting me come back a week early, as long as I participate in a work study program when I get back."

"I'm really happy for you. Let's celebrate."

"Okay. But, let me choose what we do tonight."

"Sounds good to me."

22

TYING UP LOOSE ENDS

Our bellies were full of Amy Ruth's soul food. Our minds were full of images we saw at the Brooklyn Museum exhibit. We were given a private tour by the museum curator, the woman I'd met at Ty's place. I couldn't have asked for a better afternoon.

Stephen and I arrived at Ice at eleven PM.

"Gia, you do know that I'm only nineteen, right? I thought you had to be twenty-one to get into clubs in New York." Stephen looked like a kid who just stole something.

"Just follow me, and wipe that deer-in-the-headlights look off your face." He tightened his lips, narrowed his eyes, and straightened his back.

"There you go," I nodded and smiled.

"Hey, stranger." I said to Brock, standing on my toes to give him a kiss on the cheek.

"Gia. I missed you, girl. You look a lot better since the last time I saw you."

"Yeah, I hope so."

"This is Stephen." Brock extended his hand and shook Stephen's. Stephen tightened his jaw and his hand turned red underneath his light-brown skin.

"You guys have fun tonight."

"We're not staying long, but thanks. And thanks for everything." He patted me on the back as I walked inside.

I spotted Ty's long locks cascading down his back. He was sitting at the bar having a drink. I walked to the bar, and Stephen followed. I stopped a few feet away from Ty.

"Hey, Stephen, I have a little business to handle. Can you order me a gingerale? I'll be over in a second." Stephen nodded and headed to the bar. Ty must have sensed that someone was behind him. He swiveled around on his barstool. The bags under his eyes were settled and unpacked as if they planned on hanging around. His cheeks were sunken in, and his skin was taut.

"Hey, Ty."

"Gia. I have your money. I would never shortchange you, ma," he said. He was in true form, getting straight to business.

"I know that, Ty. I tried calling you, but you shut off my phone."

"I –" I interrupted him.

"Listen, Ty. What you do in your personal life is your business. Have I ever done anything to make you think that this was anything more than a business relationship?"

He shook his head no shamefully. I felt relieved now knowing he didn't know that, at one point, I was interested in something more.

"I reacted out of surprise, Ty. Between what happened the night before and then walking in on you and –"

"Shhh." He looked around to make sure no one heard what I was saying.

"Don't worry, Ty. Your secret's safe with me."

"Yeah, I'm just starting to wonder how much longer I can keep it." He sighed in distress. He pulled an envelope out of his wallet. "It's all in there, $300."

I hugged him and held the embrace longer than usual. Some of the tension fell from his shoulders.

"Ty, if it wasn't for you giving me this job, I'm not sure what I would have done."

"When will you be back from school, Gia?"

I was so anxious to get back *to* school that I hadn't really considered if I'd come back for the summer.

"I'm not sure. I think I may try to stay on campus and take classes over the summer."

"Well, you have my number. Anytime you need a job, call me, Gia. Your work ethic and hustle is unlike anything I've ever seen."

"Well, I learned from the best." I playfully tapped him on the shoulder.

"Yeah, well, promise you won't forget me when you devour your way to the top."

"I promise. Take care of yourself, Ty." I gave him another hug.

"You too, G." He smiled.

I joined Stephen on the other side of the bar. I took a sip of my gingerale.

"Do you dance, Gia?"

"Do you?" I laughed.

"What's so funny? Is it so hard to believe that I can dance?"

"Actions speak louder than words, Stephen."

He took a gulp of his drink and pulled me to the dance floor. The DJ played some old-school *Kiss* by Prince. Stephen's dance moves surprised me. He was a great dancer. He showed off some moves and pulled me close. I swayed my hips and threw my arms around his neck. He let me lead. We sang along to the lyrics.

Stephen's dancing was much better than his singing. I laughed louder than the music, moved my hands from his neck to the back of his head, and kissed him. He stood frozen and grabbed my waist tighter. He kissed me back and the song changed, reminding me we were in the middle of the dance floor.

"Sorry," I said, embarrassed.

"Don't be. I've been waiting to kiss you ever since our lips last parted that day in the library."

"Let's get out of here." I was ready to leave.

Stephen grabbed my hand and we left the club.

****

I was excited to get back to school, but there was something I felt like I needed to do before I left.

I took the train to 168th Street. Something Micah said had stuck with me the last couple days. Because he'd be in jail for the next ten years, he'd miss the pregnancy and the first years of his child's life. I loved Micah. I knew he was a good person and would be a great father. I hoped his daughter wouldn't hold his mistakes against him.

I couldn't help but think maybe the same was true about my mother. I didn't go to the hospital expecting some grand reunion or reconciliation. I felt like I was ready to hear my mother's side of the story, or at least a portion of it.

"Next!" the security guard yelled from behind the counter.

"Hi. I'm here to see Keyshia Mahoney." He typed my mother's name into the computer and handed me a visitor's pass.

"Room 827."

The hospital smelled like ammonia and sickness. Equipment beeped and exhaled, alerting nurses and doctors to changes in vital signs. Like the machines, I took a deep breath and opened the door to Room 827.

She had the covers pulled up to her neck. I saw the silhouette of her bony frame beneath the crisp, white sheet. It reminded me of the sheet paramedics draped over dead bodies when they cart them to an ambulance. My feet felt heavy as I shuffled to her bedside.

Her eyes were shut. The skin on her face was pruny and ashen. I touched it carefully and she spasmed, forcing me to jump.

"Tangia?" She squinted. Her scratchy voice sounded as if her throat had been scraped by hundreds of shards of Plexiglas.

"Yeah, it's me."

"Tangia?" she repeated in disbelief.

"Yeah, it's me," I repeated, moving closer.

She moved her hand from underneath the sheet and waved it around, trying to find mine. I looked down at my hand and back at hers. I grabbed the metal safety rail. She must have felt the bed move when I touched the bar. She ran her hand across it until she found mine.

She had the hands of a seventy-year-old and she was only thirty-six. Her hands looked and felt like they needed a drink. Her bones poked at her skin like they were trying to escape. She coughed and wheezed.

I pressed a button on the remote on her bed to alert the nurse.

"Are you okay?" I asked moving closer, as if that, in some way, would help her stop coughing. It didn't.

"Keyshia. You all right?" I turned around at the sound of the nurse's voice. She came to the side of the bed and put what I assumed was an oxygen mask around her mouth and nose. She slowly stopped coughing. The nurse looked across the bed and smiled at me.

I faked a smile back. After my mother took a few deep breaths, the nurse removed the mask from her face.

"How's that, Keyshia?" My mother nodded and pointed to me, forming her mouth into as much of smile as the weakened muscles of her face allowed.

"Is this Gia?" the nurse asked. My mother nodded again and turned her head toward me. "Your mother has not stopped talking about you since she got here. 'My daughter Gia's in college. My daughter Gia's gonna make something of herself.' We didn't think we'd ever meet you. Good to see you. I think your mother's happy to see you too. Keyshia, call me if you need anything."

A man in a white coat walked in as the nurse left.

"Hi, Keyshia. How are we feeling today?" She nodded, smiled, and pointed to me. The coughing must have knocked the wind out of her, because she hadn't said a word since.

"You must be Gia." He checked the machines that were supporting my mother.

"Yeah. Are you my mother's doctor?"

"Sure am. Nice to meet you."

"You too. So…um…is she going to be okay?"

He looked at my mother. "Keyshia, is it okay for me to discuss your personal information with your daughter?"

She nodded and squeezed my hand.

"Well, when your mother came to us about a week ago, she wasn't in the best of shape. She lost a lot of blood from the miscarriage. Her T-cell count is low, and she has an upper respiratory infection."

"T-cell count," I said just above a whisper. The miscarriage didn't shock me as much as the mention of the T-cell count did. As harsh as it sounds, the miscarriage was somewhat of a relief. My mother was in no condition to bring another child into the world.

Although I knew what he was going to say next, I wasn't really ready to hear it.

"Gia. Your mother is HIV-positive."

I let go of my mother's hand and grabbed the bar with both hands, feeling faint. I swallowed hard and looked at my mother. Tears streamed down her face. My throat tightened. I blinked furiously, hoping that my eyelids would act as dams for the water that was attempting to escape. I looked away from my mother.

"Will she be okay?" I sniffled, thinking that was a stupid question.

"She's a fighter. Her infection seems to be clearing up, and we hope to discharge her in the next couple of days, but she won't be going home."

"She won't?"

"No. Your mother has agreed to enter a drug rehab program. When I discharge her, she'll be going to New Beginnings in Westchester County." He flipped through the pages of my mother's chart.

I looked back down at my mother. "Is that true, Keyshia? You really want to get clean?"

"I'm sorry for all the pain I put you through all these years. I was not a good mother to you. But, you were so strong, and you taught me that I can be strong too."

Tears flowed freely down my face and wet the blanket covering her. She wiped the tears from my eyes.

"It was nice to meet you, Gia," the doctor said, closing the door behind him as he left.

"I'm leaving the city this week," I said between sniffles. "I'll come back to see you tomorrow."

She nodded and closed her eyes.

"I'm going to let you get some rest." She grabbed my hand and tugged me close. She used all her energy to lift her head to kiss my cheek. I couldn't remember the last time my mother kissed me.

"I love you," she whispered. I nodded and let go of her hand. I waved goodbye as I rose to leave.

I was surprised I didn't put a hole in the mattress when I fell onto the bed in the hotel. I felt like I was carrying a huge weight on my shoulders. I sat back up and looked at the items I purchased from Duane Reade after I left the hospital.

I pulled out a small paintbrush, Elmer's glue, and a paint-by-numbers kit. I threw out the wooden kitten template, whose body was covered in tiny, inked numbers, and set the paint on the nightstand beside the bed next to the paintbrush and glue.

The red light on the phone blinked and I checked my messages.

"Hey, Gia. It's Stephen. Just calling to see if you want to grab some dinner later. Call me."

I held down the receiver, waited to hear a dial tone, and dialed Stephen's number.

"Hello?"

"Hey, Stephen."

"Hey, Gia. How was your day?"

"It was okay," I said flatly. Stephen and I were getting closer, but we weren't *that* close. I wasn't about to tell him everything I had just learned about my mother. That's when it hit me.

"Are you hungry?" he asked.

"Stephen, I need to call you back." I rushed off the phone. I thought back to the conversation I had with the doctor. My mother was HIV-positive. I was born a crack baby. My mother was shooting dope while she was pregnant with me. Was it possible that she had contacted HIV more than eighteen years ago? Was it possible to live with HIV for eighteen years without taking medication? The doctor *did* say she was a fighter. Was it possible that I could have contracted HIV from my mother as an infant?

I stood up and paced back and forth. I laughed nervously, thinking it was impossible. I was eighteen years old and had never been seriously ill. There had to be some kind of symptoms over the course of eighteen years. I couldn't possibly have HIV. Could I?

I considered going to a local clinic to get a rapid HIV test. I'd be in and out and have the results in thirty minutes. I sat back on the bed, hugged my trembling legs, and took a deep breath. Another nervous laugh escaped. I decided I was being irrational.

I took the complimentary newspaper that was left in front of the door and spread a couple of sheets over the desk. I organized the glue and painting supplies I bought from Duane Reade and started on my project.

****

I fell asleep for two hours after staring at the ceiling above my bed for most of the night.

I showered, got dressed, and headed to the business center to do a little research. I found a free HIV testing facility in Union Square. I got on the train and headed downtown.

The ten-minute train ride felt like ten hours. I kept my head down out of fear that someone would recognize me, get off at the same stop, and see that I was going into a clinic to get an HIV test. I looked out of the train window at the graffiti on the walls of the subway tunnels. I always wondered how people managed to get into the tunnels. And what was the point? To tag a name that the average person wouldn't read or even see? I got angry.

There were people who had unprotected sex with multiple partners. I never had any kind of sex with anyone. People shared needles when they shot up. So why was I, someone who always took the high road and did the right thing, going to get an HIV test? I was another example of bad things happening to good people.

I sat in a crowded waiting room with my head down. Although the clinic offered more than HIV testing, I felt as if I had a huge stamp on my forehead letting everyone else in the waiting room know why I was there.

After a grueling forty-five minute wait, a woman in scrubs called me into one of the rooms.

"Hi, Gia. Please have a seat."

"I'd really prefer to stand." I looked around the room. "Will this take long?"

"Well, the test itself doesn't take very long. However, there are a few questions I need to ask you first."

I sighed, rolled my eyes, and sat down.

"So, Gia," she looked down at a blank chart. "Tell me why you're here today."

"Well, I need to get an HIV test," I said just above a whisper, as if someone walking by would hear me.

"Okay." She wrote something on the chart.

"Listen, maybe I can save you a lot of time. I just found out my mother is HIV-positive. She did drugs while she was pregnant with me. I really don't know if she had HIV when she gave birth to me or if she contracted it recently. So, I'm here because I couldn't sleep last night, thinking there might be a small possibility that I could have HIV."

She looked up from the chart. "You made a great decision, Gia."

"Thanks." I slumped over in my seat.

"Now," she looked back down at the chart. There are several questions I need to ask you.

"Okay." I figured the less I protested, the quicker it could all be over.

"Great. Now have you ever been tested for HIV?"

"No, this is my first time."

"Okay. Are you currently, or have you been, sexually active?"

"No. Never."

"Including oral and anal sex."

I twisted up my face in disgust and repeated, "No sex in

any way, shape, or form. Ever."

"Okay. Have you ever used intravenous drugs?"

"Definitely not."

"Have you ever been diagnosed with any sexually trans-mitted infection?"

"Well, I guess that might be impossible seeing as I have never had sex." I was getting irritated fast.

"Well, unfortunately, sometimes mothers can pass not only HIV to their newborns, but also other STDs, such as herpes or syphilis."

"Well, no. I don't have any of those."

"Okay, wonderful. So, I'm going to take a swab from the inside of your cheek. I'll have you wait in the waiting room, and then I'll call you back in several minutes to discuss your results."

"Okay."

Again, twenty minutes felt like twenty hours. I looked around the room at all the young women who sat waiting. Some had young children; some didn't. They all had some-thing in common. There were no men with them. There were no men in the waiting room at all. I wished I could tell them there was so much more out there. I kept my mouth shut and figured, like me, they'd need to find that out on their own.

I was called back into the same room.

"Your test came back negative." I smiled and exhaled. "It's really rare that someone your age would exhibit no signs or symptoms eighteen years after being infected with HIV. It's very true that most people who contact HIV are asymptom-atic, meaning they have no symptoms, but to show no symp-toms without taking medication after eighteen years, I would say is pretty rare. I think it was very smart and responsible of you to come in. I'd normally set up a follow-up appointment for three months from now, but in your case, there's really no need to do that."

"Okay. Thank you."

"Take care of yourself, Gia. Best of luck to you." She smiled.

I wasn't sure what she was wishing me luck for, but I thanked her anyway.

✱✱

The blinking red light on the phone illuminated a narrow corner of the room. I knew the messages were from Stephen. He called several times after I hung up last night. I'd let the phone ring without answering.

"Hi, Gia. It's Stephen. You hung up so quickly. I'm just calling to make sure everything is all right. Please call me when you get this message."

"Hey, Gia it's Stephen again. Well, I guess we won't be going to dinner tonight. Just call me and let me know what time you want to head back to Rhode Island tomorrow."

Was it really Monday already? I looked around the room for a calendar. There wasn't one.

"Hey, Gia. It's Stephen. Call me so we can make the arrangements for tomorrow."

I finally called Stephen back.

"Hello?"

"Hi, Stephen. Did I wake you?"

"It's okay." He cleared his voice. "Please tell me you're still in the city.

"Yeah, I'm still here."

"I thought you left. Trying to find you is like trying to find Waldo. I called you a million times last night. You were supposed to go back to school yesterday. Where were you?"

"I had something I needed to take care of. Listen, Stephen. I'm not ready to go back to school yet."

"What? But I thought you were dying to get back?"

"I was. Well, I am. But, there are some things I need to

take care of here first. I won't be ready to leave until the end of the week."

"The end of the week?" He sounded worried.

"Yeah. And, when we go back to school, I should have a check for $1,500 waiting for me there. I plan on paying you back every penny for the hotel bill."

"Don't worry about it. I like that I'm able to help you."

"Well, I appreciate your help, but I want to pay you back. You're planning to go back home before you go back to school, right?"

"Yeah. I was going to leave with you today. But, if you're not ready to leave, I can–"

"Stephen, that's not really necessary. I can make it back to school on my own. Please go home. I'll see you over the weekend back on campus."

"I'm not so sure I'm ready to leave New York yet. I like it here. Do you mind if I stay until the end of the week?"

"Stephen, you can do whatever you want. I'm just letting you know that, over the next couple of days, there are some really personal things I need to handle."

"I understand. I'd still prefer to hang around, but I'll give you all the space you need."

"Okay," I said, secretly happy that Stephen was staying.

"So, I know I just told you I'd give you your space, but do you have plans for lunch?"

"I was planning on going to Westchester today. I need to go see my brother."

"Okay." He tried to mask his disappointment.

"Would you mind if we grabbed something to eat in West-chester?"

"That would be great. Let me get dressed, and I'll swing by to get you in about an hour." His voice brightened with excitement.

"Is it okay if it's a late lunch, Stephen? I don't want to miss visiting hours."

"That's fine. I'll just eat some breakfast before I head out."

"That's not a bad idea. I'll do the same."

"Okay, Gia. I'll see you soon."

"Bye."

I appreciated the ride to Westchester, but was worried Stephen would ask to come inside with me. I considered introducing him to Micah but decided against it. That would be too much too soon, and I wasn't ready for all of that.

"I shouldn't be long," I said while getting out of the car.

"Take your time. I'm not going anywhere. I'm not trying to go to lunch without my date." He smiled

"I won't be long." I smiled back.

When I visited Micah, I usually drew stares or received attention from the other inmates. But that day was different. Many pointed at me. Some even pointed me out to their visitors. I put my head down, thinking that maybe the bruises on my face didn't heal as well as I thought. There was a huge grin on Micah's face when I met him at the table.

"My little sis, the superstar!" He hugged me.

"Micah, what are you talking about?" I looked around at the others in the room who were still staring.

"You didn't even see it yet, did you?"

"See what, Mich?"

"The Jahzelle video."

"What?" I asked. "It's out already?"

"You haven't seen it yet? You're a star, G. I almost didn't recognize you. You looking all done up and grown in the video."

"Well, I guess that explains why everyone is looking at me." I scanned the room.

"Yeah, and they need to take they eyes off my little sister," he yelled. After he said it, some looked away, while others continued to gawk.

"So, how are you, Micah?"

He was about to answer when he looked behind me. A huge grin spread across his face. I followed his glance. There was a woman walking in our direction. She was as tall as me but thinner, except for the small bump in her stomach. Micah got up from his seat and pulled out the chair next to me. He kissed the woman on her cheek and held her hand as she sat down.

"Gia, this is my girl, Sophie. And, this is my little girl, Zoey," he said, touching her stomach.

"Hi, I'm Gia." I extended my hand.

"Gia, I feel like I know you as much as Micah talks about you." She leaned in a little closer. "Hold up. Aren't you the girl from the Jahzelle video?"

"Yeah." I looked down at my feet. I wasn't sure of how to handle this. I was also embarrassed that I didn't know as much about her as she did about me.

"Okay," she said, smiling.

"So, how you feeling, Sophie?" Micah asked.

"I'm good. I went to the doctor last week. He said everything looks good. The baby's healthy. I'll get another sonogram next month."

"Word? Wish I could be there with you to see it." He sounded disappointed.

"Mich, you'll be out of here in no time."

The time flew by, as with all of my visits with Micah. It was especially short this time, because I had to share the visit with Sophie.

"Aight, Micah. I won't see you again for a while. I'm headed back to school at the end of the week."

"Aight, G. Take care of yourself." He hugged me. "Make me proud, girl."

"I'll try. I promise to write, and I'll try to send a new poem every week. I love you, Mich."

"Oh, hold up, G. Speaking of poems." He reached into this back pocket, cleared his throat, and began to read.

A great man once said,
That life ain't no crystal stair.
And these sure ain't no crystal bars
That I'm trapped behind.
They . . . They're cold and metal,
Got a brother locked up and locked down.
But I got to look up and not down,
Drawing on the strength of these bars,
I can strengthen myself while I'm behind them,
Learning from my mistakes.
So I can be a better man,
A good dad, and be a light
For my growing seed.

He folded up the paper and handed it to me.

"I know you always say poems ain't gotta rhyme so—"

"Mich, I'm speechless. You wrote that, Mich?" My voice was raspy, and I was holding back tears.

"Yeah, G. I couldn't have done it without you."

I unfolded the paper and ran my finger over the lines of the poem.

"I love you, Mich." I placed the poem in my purse.

"I love you too, G." I stepped away and let Micah say goodbye to Sophie. When they finished saying their good-byes, she walked toward me.

"Do you want a ride back to the city, Sophie?" I asked.

"Yeah, definitely. Do you have a car?"

"My friend does. He's waiting outside."

"Okay." We walked to the exit together, and I looked down at the Duane Reade bag in my hand.

"Oh, hold on a second, Sophie." I turned back toward Micah.

"Micah!" I called from across the room. He stopped and turned. I ran to him and took the jewelry box out of the bag. I'd painted over the ballerina's rust spots and glued her arm back on.

"I wanted to give you this to hold onto. My grandmother gave it to me, and I want to give it to you to give to your little girl. It's been through a lot and doesn't play music very well anymore, but it'll look really pretty in her room. And if she takes really good care of it, maybe she can pass it on to her daughter someday."

"Gia, this is beautiful." He admired the jewelry box.

"Yeah, it really means a lot to me. So take good care of it, so you can give it to her when the time's right."

He hugged me, and I held on a little tighter and longer than usual, knowing it would be at least five months before I'd see him again.

I watched him walk back with the other inmates, the ballerina jewelry box in his hand. I turned around and walked out with Sophie.

23

CAN'T TEACH AN OLD DOG NEW TRICKS

The doctor was on his way out as I was on my way in.

"Hi, Gia. How are you this morning?"

"I'm okay. Will she be discharged today?"

"She's doing well, but I'd really like to wait one more day to release her. Discharge is at eleven tomorrow morning."

"Is she still going to the rehab center?"

"She is. Hasn't changed her mind." He smiled. "They have someone coming here to meet her at her time of discharge."

"Okay. Thank you." He nodded and left the room.

My mother sat up in her bed. The life was back in her face. Maury Povich was on a television perched in the corner of the room.

"You are *not* the father!" she yelled, pointing her bony finger at the television and laughing. Her laugh quickly turned into a nasty cough. I grabbed a clean bedpan from a cart and held it to her mouth so she could spit in it. I turned away in disgust when she did. When she was finished, I placed the bedpan on the floor and kicked it toward the bathroom.

"Thanks, Gia." She wiped the remaining spit off of her

mouth with the back of her hand. "Sit down." She pointed to the chair on the other side of the bed.

"No. I'm not really going to stay all that long. I have some things I need to do before I go back to school."

"Your mama ain't more important than getting ready to go back to school?" She cut her eyes at me and then back at Maury Povich. She had the attention span of a five-year-old. "This show is a trip, boy! These women crazy not knowin' who they baby's daddies is."

"Yeah. They're a trip." I looked at her, thinking the only difference between her and those women was that she didn't air out her dirty laundry on television. It was still just as dirty and smelled just as bad.

"So, you getting out of this place tomorrow?" I looked around the room.

"Yeah. I'll be heading up to Westchester tomorrow."

"They're coming to get you at eleven."

"That's what they say." Her attention was still on Maury.

"Okay, well, I'll be back tomorrow at eleven."

"Okay. Nice of you to stop by and see me today." I couldn't tell if she was being sincere or sarcastic.

"Okay, Key..., Mom. I'll see you tomorrow."

****

When I arrived at my mother's apartment, there were no men sitting on the couch drinking beers, but the empty beer bottles were still there, along with all the rest of the same mess that was there the last time I was.

I put down a bag of cleaning supplies and thought about where I should start. I began picking up the dirty clothes strewn all over the apartment. I shoved them inside of two large garbage bags and took them down to the laundry room. I left them in the washer and returned to the apartment to continue cleaning.

Now that I could actually see the floor, it was easier to move around the apartment. I threw away twenty beer bottles that littered every room of the apartment.

I pulled out a pair of thick, yellow dishwashing gloves from the shopping bag. I took the plates out of the sink and stacked them on the kitchen counter. As the plates and glasses started to shift, so did the roaches. They crawled out of glasses that contained sticky remnants of Kool-Aid and Coca-Cola. Some floated lifelessly inside of bowls half full of lumpy, old, sour milk. I killed as many of the live ones as I could with my fist.

Once all of the dishes were out of the sink and organized on the counter, I sprayed the sink with bleach, wiped it clean and free of roaches, and filled it with soapy water.

Once the dishes were done, I ran back down to the laundry room and threw the clothes into the dryer. By the time I got back into the apartment, the dishes were somewhat dry. I dried the remaining spots of water off with a clean dishrag. I sprayed the counters down with bleach and covered the corners with boric acid.

I swept the floors and mopped them as best I could. I went into my room and straightened up the things that my mother had thrown around. I went into her room and did the same. As I made her bed, I stopped and picked up a picture that was on the nightstand. It was a picture of her holding me in the hospital when I was a newborn. The picture looked as if it had been folded several times. There were white cracks that traveled the entire surface of the picture, and the colors were faded. For the most part, it was still intact. I folded it along a few of its many creases and put it in my back pocket.

Now that I had cleaned most of the apartment, I took a deep breath and prepared to clean the bathroom. The cover to the toilet was down. I covered my nose with my forearm and held my breath. It hadn't been flushed in days. I flushed it with my available arm, looked away, and gagged. My eyes watered.

I sprayed air freshener and decided to clean the tub first. There was a ring of dirt around it and the shower curtain was covered in mold. It wasn't worth cleaning. I ripped it down and tossed it into a garbage bag. I'd have to go back to the dollar store the following day to buy a new one.

After cleaning the entire bathroom, I cracked the window because the fumes from the bleach were causing my throat and eyes to burn. I welcomed the overpowering smell of the bleach. It was much better than the *other* smell I encountered when I first started cleaning.

I took two large garbage bags to the incinerator down the hall. I went down to the laundry room, took the clothes out of the dryer, and folded them. I went back upstairs and used the shopping bag from the cleaning supplies to carry my mother's belongings in. I purchased her a toothbrush, toothpaste, soap, and lotion from the dollar store. I added a couple of pairs of pajamas, pants, shirts, and underwear to the bag. I removed the picture I found on the nightstand from my back pocket and placed it in the bag. I looked around the apartment, turned off the lights, and locked the door.

When I arrived at the hospital at 10:30 the next morning, there was a nurse's aid making my mother's bed.

"Did I miss her?" I looked down at my watch.

"We all did," the woman who made the bed said, looking up at me.

"What are you talking about?"

"She left sometime last night. No one saw her go," a voice coming from behind me answered. It was the nurse I met the first time I came to visit. She walked in with another woman I didn't know.

"What?" I asked.

"Gia, this is the social worker. She's from the rehab center in Westchester that your mother was supposed to go to." The nurse introduced me to the woman beside her.

"Hey." The social worker extended her hand. I grabbed it with the tips of my fingers and shook without much effort. "I was really looking forward to meeting your mother, but I'd be lying if I said this was the first time I've seen something like this happen. It's pretty typical. In a moment of desperation and intense emotion, an addict will agree to treatment, and when the urge gets too strong for her to handle, she bails."

I looked down at the bag in my hand.

"I get it. Excuse me."

I walked over to a small trash can at the end of the bed. I threw the bag of my mother's belongings inside and walked out.

When I returned to my hotel room, the red light on the phone was blinking. I assumed it was Stephen.

"Hi, Gia. It's Stephen. Call me when you get in."

I called him back immediately this time.

"Hello?"

"Hey, Stephen. It's Gia. Listen, I'm going to check out of the hotel tomorrow. I'm heading back to Rhode Island."

"But I thought —"

I interrupted him. "But, you thought wrong, Stephen!" I tried to hold back my tears, but like ice under the pressure of a hot liquid, I cracked.

"Are you okay?"

I wiped the tears from my eyes and the snot from my nose. "So, checkout is at eleven AM. I think. If you try to call, I won't be here."

"Wait. Slow down. What happened to staying in New York for a couple more days?"

"Plans change, Stephen."

"Okay, Gia. I'll be at the hotel tomorrow to pick you up."

"Stephen, I'm taking the bus back."

"What? Why would you even do that? It's so unnecessary, Gia. I can–"

"Stephen!" I screamed. "I'll see you when the semester starts, and I'll have every penny of your money." I slammed down the phone. I rolled over onto my belly and pounded my fists into the pillows as if they were the ones who'd hurt me.

"I hate you!" I screamed to the empty room. Tears stormed out of my eyes. I felt like I'd suffocate in the wet blankets. Fragments of my life unspooled in my mind with movie trailer speed.

My grandmother brushed my hair into braided ponytails. She gave me a bath.

My mother shot up on the toilet in the bathroom. She sold my talking teddy bear to a man outside of a crack house. I felt the cold of the bricks I sat on while waiting outside for her as she got high.

I remembered Micah touching Zoey through Sophie's belly. At some point unknown to me, these visions meshed with my dreams, and I fell fast asleep.

I woke up to the sound of someone pounding on the door. I looked at the alarm clock on the nightstand. It was seven AM. I got up and looked through the peephole. It was Stephen. I unbolted and unchained the door.

"I know that you don't really want to see me but–"

"Stephen, come in."

He sat on the desk with one foot on the floor.

"Listen, I'm really sorry for the way I've treated you. I've blown you off since we met, and all you ever wanted to do was help me. I'm just so used to doing things on my own that–"

I felt the tears rolling down my face. He joined me on the edge of the bed and put one hand on my shoulder, using the other to wipe my tears.

"Stephen, when you're away at school, do you ever get

homesick?"

He took his arm from my shoulder and searched my face as if the answer was there.

"Don't give me the answer I want to hear. Just be straight with me."

"Sometimes yes and sometimes no. I have a great family. I do know how fortunate I am to have them."

"Yeah, you are."

"Just because you don't have the greatest family doesn't mean you don't have people who love you." He lifted my chin with his finger in one delicate motion and kissed me.

"Stephen?"

"Yeah," he said anxiously.

"I'm really, *really* hungry." I laughed.

"I'd thought you'd never ask. Come on." He pulled me up from the bed, and we headed downstairs to have breakfast.

We talked about Stephen's plans to study abroad in the spring and my plans to actually choose a major in the upcoming semester. I didn't tell Stephen what happened during the previous forty-eight hours. Something told me that Stephen and I would be friends for a long time, and I'd tell him when the time was right.

"It's getting late. I need to check out by eleven."

"You know, you can stay until Friday. Don't worry about the money."

"Thanks, Stephen. But it's more than just the money. It's time to get back to school. I came here and did what I needed to do. But now it's time to get back to what I've been working for my whole life."

"I understand. Because you're returning early, will you have to pay?"

"Yeah, but they officially open the dorms back up on Friday. The work study offer no longer stands, but I'll only have to pay for two nights. And, Residence Life agreed to charge it to my account."

"Okay. And you're sure you don't need a ride back?"

"I appreciate the offer, but I really need to go back on my own. You've done so much for me, Stephen. I'm beyond grateful. But I need to ride back to school alone. There's a lot I need to process before I start the semester."

"I understand. Can I see you when we get back to school?"

"Of course. I look forward to it." I put my hand on his knee.

"I got you something, Gia." He pulled out a wrapped package from a shopping bag.

"What is it?"

"I'm not telling you. Open it on your way back to school."

"You didn't have to get me a gift." I ran my finger over the beautiful wrapping paper.

"I know I didn't have to. I wanted to. Can I at least drive you to the bus station?"

"Okay." I smiled.

24

GOING BACK

packed my things and checked out of the hotel. The bill came to $1,890. I promised Stephen $1,500 of it as soon as I received my check from the video shoot. The rest of the balance I'd pay off in smaller payments. Stephen told me not to worry about it. I insisted on paying him back.

On the way to the bus station, Stephen tried to convince me to let him drive me back to school. After declining his offer three times, he offered to pay for my bus ticket home. I refused.

I placed my duffel bag underneath the bus and took my purse and Stephen's gift onboard with me. I opened the wrapping paper, trying not to rip it. It was a beautiful locket. It was large and round with a carving of a ballerina on it. I opened it. There was a picture of us that one of Stephen's friends snapped at the campus cafeteria. Originally, we weren't the only ones in the picture. It was obvious Stephen had cut the others out. I laughed and shook my head. The side opposite the picture read "1 Corinthians 13." I looked out the window, confused. I knew it was a reference to the Bible, but had no idea what it said. I figured I'd look it up once I got back to school.

I placed the locket back inside of the box. As I did, the cotton shifted, revealing a small card. My name was written on the outside of the card. Inside it read:

1 Corinthians 13
Love is patient,
Love is kind.
It does not envy,
It does not boast,
It is not proud.
It does not dishonor others,
It is not self-seeking,
It is not easily angered,
It keeps no recorders of wrongs . . .
It always protects, always trusts, always hopes, always preserves.
Love never fails.
And now these three things remain: faith, hope and love,
But the greatest of these is love.

Gia,
I love you in the truest sense of the word. I look forward to falling deeper in love with you and pray that, one day, you might feel the same way about me.
Love,
Stephen

I took the locket back out of the box and placed it around my neck. I looked out the window as the bus pulled out of the terminal. The surrounding buildings became blurred as my eyes filled with tears. I closed my eyes and allowed them to flow.

My future lay ahead of me, several hours away. Behind me

was everything that, at one time, I was so anxious to leave behind. I was excited for what lay ahead but was grateful for the lessons I learned at home.

ACKNOWLEDGMENTS

None of this would have been possible without God. I'm far from perfect, yet your love is unconditional. For that I am forever grateful.

To my mother Wanda. You are an amazing mother and my best friend. Words cannot describe how much I appreciate all of your love and support. You are my rock. I feel privileged to call you mom. To my father John who has never referred to me as his stepdaughter. I may not be yours biologically, but you are my dad and I am your daughter. I love you. To my boo boo Josh. I've adored you since the day you were born. Even though you're taller than me, you'll always be my little brother.

To the Forbes women. Grandma you would (and have) literally given me the shirt off of your back. Our beautiful family was built from your strength. I love you immensely. Aunt Dawn you are like a second mother to me. Your support is incredible. Aunt Jackie I could not ask for a better aunt. You always make me laugh and have always been there for me.

To my cousins. We grew up together and as adults, I'm proud to call you friends. Jocie, Nell, EB, Jinesa, Angie, Toni, Dave, Maury and Mikey (RIP). To my younger cousins I love you all so much. I pray that I can be a good role model to all of you.

To my Aunt Clyde and Uncle Junie. I love you guys. Uncle June, you have always been like a father to me. I can't thank you enough.

To my sister Veronica. You've grown up to be an incredible young woman. I look forward to getting to know you better.

To my girls- Chante, Josephine, Kira, Yesenia, Olivia and Nicole. I love you girls like sisters. Jamillah you are one of the few people who asked to read my manuscript and actually read it in its entirety. Thank you.

To Talia Culley. Thank you for doing a beautiful job on my makeup for my back cover photo. You truly are an artist.

To my students. Binta, Jessica, Genesis, Malika and Xiao. Thank you for all your feedback. You will always be remembered as the members of my very first book club. You girls are awesome.

To Professor Bens at Manhattanville College. Home Sick started as a short story for your narrative writing class. You read it and told me it should be a novel. You also gave me very honest feedback as to what worked and what was trash. I'm not sure if this would have ever become a novel if it weren't for your class. Thank you.

To my editor Chris Guthrie at Open Book Editors. Thanks for your editing services, honest feedback and availability in answering my many questions.

To Lora Morgenstern. Thank you for designing some of the most important parts of my books. It's clear the book was designed by a professional. You are creative, diligent, patient and kind. It was a pleasure working with you.

To my writing group. Because you're all such great writers, I value your feedback. You all are brutally honest yet encouraging. Thanks for that.

To Julia Alverez, Claude McKay, Langston Hughes and Maya Angelou. Your poetry is beautiful, moving, and inspires me to be a better writer and human being.

To the city of New York. If you were a man, I'd marry you. You're the city I love to hate. You've made me who I am. Thank you.

APPENDIX- POETRY CITED

1. Ironing Their Clothes- Julia Alvarez Homecoming: New and Collected Poems (New York: Plume, 1996).

2. Tropics in New York- Claude McKay- Copyright unknown.

3. Mother to Son – Langston Hughes Published 1922

4. Kid in the Park- Langston Hughes (Knopf, 1959).

5. Caged Bird- Maya Angelou Published 1969

ABOUT THE AUTHOR

Jessica Harris is a teacher at a New York City public high school. She enjoys writing both fiction and poetry. Her poetry placed in the 78th Annual Writer's Digest Writing Competition and she won Manhattanville College's Robert O'Clair poetry award in 2003. Jessica currently resides in Brooklyn, New York. *Home'Sick* is her first novel.

jessica.loretta.harris@gmail.com
jessicalorettaharris.com

www.ingramcontent.com/pod-product-compliance
Lightning Source LLC
Chambersburg PA
CBHW030247200626
46816CB00002BA/544